Simone's heartbeats increased to a treacherous level. She had a feeling she wasn't going to like what he had to say next. He wasn't talking about money here; it was something far more dangerous.

'So what is it exactly you want from me, Cade?' she asked, when he came to a halt at her side. She could feel the heat of his skin, smell the dangerous male scent of him. Every one of her senses was on high alert.

'I'll turn your company around in return for—'

Simone knew what he was doing; he was testing her nerves, wanting to see whether she'd back out before he put any clauses into their agreement. She stood up and looked straight into his face, trying not to show the panic swirling inside her.

His golden eyes blazed into hers, claiming her, making her his before he'd even spoken. 'In return for you in bed beside me. Every night. As my mistress. No concessions. If you want to keep your business you've no choice.'

Dear Reader

100 years of Mills & Boon! I can't help but wonder how many titles have been published in that time, and I'm proud to be a part of this phenomenon in romantic fiction. I was first published in 1976, and had the honour of dining with Alan Boon at the GPO Tower in London. I received a Certificate of Orbit, on which Alan wrote, *'I much enjoyed our high-level talks—and look forward to the result.'* The result is thirty-two years of writing!

This year has not only been an exciting year for Mills & Boon, but for its authors as well. We're all a part of the celebrations. Writing romance has to be the best profession in the world. I never thought when my first book was accepted that I'd still be writing now. And the sheer joy of it never goes away.

In this book, set in Australia, Cade meets up with Simone, the woman who was instrumental in him losing his inheritance, and he is determined to get his revenge. Tempers fly but, as in all good romance stories, love conquers all. It's the journey to that final declaration of love that's the all-important story. I do hope you enjoy it.

Warmest wishes

Margaret

THE BILLIONAIRE'S BLACKMAIL BARGAIN

BY
MARGARET MAYO

MILLS & BOON™
Pure reading pleasure

First published in Great Britain 2008
Harlequin Mills & Boon Limited,
Eton House, 18-24 Paradise Road, Richmond, Surrey TW9 1SR

© Margaret Mayo 2008

ISBN: 978 0 263 20324 0

Set in Times Roman 10½ on 12¾ pt
07-0708-52505

Printed and bound in Great Britain
by Antony Rowe Ltd, Chippenham, Wiltshire

Margaret Mayo was born in Staffordshire, England, and still lives within twenty miles of her childhood home. Ever since she was a child she has always loved reading, but never dreamt that one day she would write her own books. She began writing in the seventies, when an idea for a story popped into her head, and she plans to go on doing so for a very long time. She likes nothing better than to sit in her office and dream up new characters and situations.

Recent titles by the same author:

BEDDED AT HIS CONVENIENCE
THE RICH MAN'S RELUCTANT MISTRESS
BOUGHT FOR MARRIAGE

CHAPTER ONE

Simone Maxwell sat staring into space, twirling her wine glass between nerveless fingers, unaware that a good-looking man sitting on the other side of the room had been observing her closely. Outwardly she looked calm and in control, but inwardly she was seething with despair.

This was the worst day of her life. The words she had just heard from the two men seated opposite her were the death-knell to her business, which was already teetering on the edge of disaster. She did an instant replay of their conversation in her head before speaking. 'Are you sure I can't get you to change your mind?' It was a struggle to keep her voice steady.

Two heads shook in unison. Two faces were very serious. One of the men spoke. 'We're very sorry, Miss Maxwell, but it's not a sound proposition. It would simply take more money than we're prepared to invest.'

'And there's nothing I can say that will make any difference?' Simone tried to make her voice remain calm, hoping she didn't sound too anxious. She didn't want to appear as a desperate, panicking, neurotic female in front of these two men, even if that was exactly what she felt like at this precise moment.

Throughout dinner she had maintained her calm demeanour, stating her case clearly, assuring them it would be a good long-term investment. She had failed, but she was determined to try just one last time. 'Gentlemen, I'm certain that—'

'Miss Maxwell, there's nothing more you can say,' interjected the younger of her male companions. 'Like I said, we're sorry, but it's not for us.' They finished their coffee and got to their feet. 'We wish you the best of luck.' They shook hands and then quietly left the restaurant.

The best of luck! Luck didn't enter into the equation. She was done for.

The yacht-charter company meant everything to her. It had been started by her parents when she was a young girl, and her mother had run the office while her father had dealt with the practical side of things. She used to sit in the office with her mother and pretend to help, and when she had finished her education she had worked for the company full time.

Her mother had always said that one day the company would be hers, and sure enough Simone's father had handed over the reins to his daughter. But it had come with a catch. The business had been in trouble when he'd handed it over, and Simone had discovered that her father had been slowly gambling his money away, drawing more and more on the business funds. By the time Simone had discovered the extent of the problem, it had been too late. Now she found herself practically begging strangers for help, trying to salvage the business in any way she could.

Simone held her head in her hands. If only her father had been more careful with his money. If only she had seen the accounts earlier. If only. She hated her father for his selfish actions, whilst loving him at the same time as only a daughter can.

The business had meant everything to Simone's mother, and for this reason Simone was willing to do everything in her power not to let her down. She had been so proud of the success they'd had with their venture. She would be heart-broken if she knew what was happening now.

So engrossed was Simone in her thoughts that she didn't see the man crossing the room. The first she knew of his presence was when his well-remembered voice cracked open memories best forgotten.

Cade Dupont!

The last person in the world she wanted to see at a time like this. How he would glory in her downfall.

She turned her head, her breath catching in her throat, raw emotions rising like a floodtide. His six-feet-plus figure towered over her; his savagely handsome face sent a chill straight through her heart. Simone closed her eyes, hoping he was nothing more than a figment of her imagination and of deeply disturbing memories, but no—when she slanted another look, he was still there.

An impeccable grey jacket sat over wide shoulders, and matching trousers hid powerful thighs. A white silk-shirt emphasised skin darkened by the sun, and a grey-and-gold-silk tie completed his ensemble. The gold in the tie matched the gold in his eyes—eyes that once had the power to melt her bones at a hundred paces. And, unhappily, he was as gloriously male as he had ever been.

'What are you doing here?' Simone asked.

'Now there's a welcome.' Without waiting for an invitation, he slid on to a chair opposite. 'Aren't you pleased to see me?'

'I'm surprised,' she replied, ignoring his question. 'I thought you were on the other side of the world.'

'And by the look on your face you wish I'd stayed there.' His nostrils flared, and the smile that accompanied his initial greeting slammed back to wherever it had come from. His lips turned unforgivingly down at the corners, and his golden eyes cut a laser beam through the space between them. 'Tell me, what was your meeting about? You clearly didn't get what you wanted.'

Disbelief flashed in Simone's violet eyes. 'You were eavesdropping? I can't believe that—'

'Hardly,' he intervened. 'But body language is very telling, and perhaps I might be permitted to say that you still have a very fanciable body.' His eyes dropped from her face to the swell of her breasts beneath her fine cashmere top.

Simone ignored the sudden prickle of heat his hard eyes engendered; a heat that started subtly but then claimed every corner of her body until she felt as if she was on fire. 'What are you doing here, Cade—apart from spying on me, of course?' She had thought her day couldn't get any worse. Big mistake! Cade Dupont had every reason to be furious with her, but she didn't need his caustic tongue at this moment.

His dark hair with its inclination to curl was cut brutally short; she could even see the glint of a grey hair or two. And his well-defined brows levelled over eyes that were uncomfortably intent. 'I'm here on business,' he announced.

His generous mouth turned up all too briefly, and his spectacularly long-lashed eyes continued to abrade her. Eyes that used to…no! She mustn't go down that path. Not again. *Not ever!* Even though her traitorous body recognised this man as the one who had initiated her into the world of spinning senses and intensified emotions. The man who had taken her on a voyage of discovery of her own sensuality.

'Business?' she questioned when he didn't enlarge.

'Yes, I'm looking to set up a new company here.'

'Here? Right here?' Even to her own ears she sounded stupid. But what else could she say? She didn't want Cade Dupont on her doorstep again; he was her past. Part of which, even she had to admit, had been gloriously happy—even fantastically, spectacularly exciting—but it had all ended in disaster. And there was nothing she could do about it now.

'What sort of business?' she asked, in a voice that sounded nothing like her own.

The Whitsundays were Australia's premier area for boat hire. Surely he wasn't thinking of setting up in opposition to her? Trips out to the Great Barrier Reef were always booked well in advance. In fact the Whitsundays, with its more than a hundred different islands—many of them national parks, some with holiday resorts—were the jewels in the crown of any holiday destination.

Simone counted herself lucky to live in such a beautiful part of the world, but her hopes and ambitions hadn't worked out. Now the company needed a massive cash investment, money she didn't have and which the banks refused to lend her. Her last hope had been the two men who'd just left.

She threw the remains of her wine down her throat and reached for the bottle.

'Allow me.'

Long brown fingers touched hers, making her flinch and draw back. She sucked in a deep breath and blew it out again slowly. She watched as Cade refilled her glass and beckoned for one to be brought to him. He exuded confidence big-time.

Cade was thirty-two now, she was nine years younger—older and wiser than the eighteen-year-old who'd made such a fool of herself. But not old enough to handle an ailing business, she thought bitterly. Not old enough to have amassed enough money to turn it around.

It had been on a downward spiral ever since she'd taken over. It needed money for everything: essential boat mainte-nance, new boats to replace the older ones, and the fact was she simply didn't have it. Her father had handed her a sinking ship, and although Simone spent all her time trying to save the business bookings were getting fewer and fewer.

Soon she would have to call it a day. Which was a shame, because she was in a prime position. She had a good-sized marina. Someone would snap her hands off, and with the right financial investment it would garner a small fortune.

'What sort of business am I contemplating?' Cade held his glass up to the light and studied its contents as though it was of paramount importance. A small, satisfied smile settled on his lips. 'Sailing-boat charter; it's the only business I know.'

Simone felt her heart stop, and it was a long time before it started again. 'You run a charter company in England?'

Dark brows rose. 'Why not?' His nostrils dilated. His attitude changed. And his next words were clipped and precise. 'Clearly I had to get a loan, but I found the business very lucrative—run properly.' Then his golden eyes narrowed on her face. 'How is your company, by the way?'

He knew! She could tell by his challenging voice, by his closely guarded expression. He'd been asking questions. He was well aware that she now ran MM Charters and that it was on a slippery slope to humiliating failure.

'I have no wish to discuss it,' Simone replied tautly.

'No?' One eyebrow rose this time. 'Why is that, I wonder? Could it have anything to do with the fact that it's not doing too well at the moment?'

'So you were prying!' she accused, violet eyes blazing. Heavens, she needed to leave, and quickly. The middle of a restaurant was no place to argue with Cade Dupont. She sucked in another deep breath, and then another, and when he didn't respond she rose to her feet. 'I have to leave. Goodbye, Cade.'

With her back ramrod-straight and her chin high, Simone marched from the elegant dining room. But Cade wasn't letting her get away that easily. Through a mirror in the facing wall, she caught sight of him striding after her, although not before he had thrown a handful of notes on to the table.

Damn! She'd forgotten to pay. Or was it his own bill he was settling? She swung around and faced him fiercely. 'What was that money for?'

'Just settling up.'

Simone opened her bag and searched for her credit card, but a firm hand stilled her.

'My treat.'

'I won't let you,' she snapped, horrified when his touch sent her pulses into devastating spasm. She didn't need this; she didn't want personal complications on top of her present problems. Cade was her past, and that was where he must stay.

'Can you really afford to turn me down?' he asked in a silken-smooth voice, his long, hard body almost touching hers. He was so close that she could smell the male scent of him; so close that she could feel the full violent impact of his sexuality.

'And what's that supposed to mean?' Simone's enormous eyes were almost purple in her distress. She wished he would step away. She didn't want to back off, because it would reveal the fact that she found him too deeply disturbing, but his nearness threatened to cut off her breathing.

'Your problems are common knowledge around here, Simone.' He smiled as he spoke, and in her heightened state Simone felt that he was taking great delight in imparting that piece of news. 'Of course everyone's sympathetic, they know that your father is the cause of your problems, but business is business, isn't that right?' he murmured smoothly. 'And since I'm in the same game maybe there's something I can do for you?'

Simone's heartbeat quickened until finally it hammered a painful tattoo against her ribcage. She wanted to put her hand over it, still its flight, but to do so would alert Cade to her fear. What was he suggesting—that he buy her out? She couldn't allow that. It would be too ironic by far.

'There's nothing you can do, nothing I want you to do,' she declared fiercely, continuing her race out of the restaurant. 'I'll sort my own problems.'

It was bad enough that he'd paid her bill, without him offering to bail her out of her present financial difficulties. And it was extremely humiliating that he had asked around and found out how badly MM Charters was doing. She could have done with hiding that fact from him. Her situation was actually worse than anyone knew. A few more weeks, maybe less, and she would be out of business altogether.

But Cade was persistent. 'You really would be a fool to turn me down.'

He was hot on her heels as she raced out of the restaurant, and Simone fancied that she could feel his breath on the back of her neck. She hurried even faster to her parked car. It was unbelievable that he still had the power to churn her emotions. It felt as though the years in between had melted away like raindrops in the sun.

Their relationship had been hot and amorous; she'd given herself to him so completely that it was embarrassing now to even think about it. He had taught her the art of love-making. He had turned her from an innocent teenager into a woman fully aware of her body and all the pleasures it held. She had been totally in love with him.

When she reached her car she turned around, fully intending to tell him to leave her alone. But when their eyes met, when she saw the dangerous darkness lurking there, a cyclone erupted, sucking all the breath from her body. She saw once again the man who had been her perfect lover, and instead of thinking about her troubles all she could concentrate on was Cade himself and the way he could still whip up her emotions to such an extent that she wanted to scream for release.

'Please leave me alone.' Her voice was no more than a husky whisper, and she was conscious of her breasts rising and falling far more rapidly than they were supposed to. The only time they had ever behaved like this was when they'd been making spectacular, glorious love.

Simone checked her thoughts. Best not think along those lines. Not at this moment anyway. She was more concerned with getting rid of Cade.

Except that Cade did not want to go. His feet were planted firmly on the ground. He leaned on the car with one hand, and his other looked as though it was prepared to take the key fob from her if she should dare try to climb inside.

His eyes locked unwaveringly with hers. She had never met a man with eyes so sensationally golden. They were the colour of a lion's skin—sometimes softly seductive, sometimes purposeful, sometimes dark with passion. They used to turn her bones to liquid, and the annoying part was that they still had the power to thrill.

'Don't dismiss my offer out of hand, Simone,' he said softly. 'If what I've been told is true, I've arrived at exactly the right time.'

'And why would you help me?' she asked faintly.

Cade was asking himself the same question. Why would he want to help Simone when she had been instrumental in him losing his fortune? He ought to run a mile. She could deny it for as long as she liked, but Matthew Maxwell had confirmed that his daughter had known all along exactly what she was doing. He had never thought her capable of such duplicity, and his hurt had been unbearable. He should have been pleased that Simone was out of his life. But, damn it, he'd never been able to forget her. He'd enjoyed teaching her the pleasures of the flesh, and she'd become a sensational lover. He'd thought she was the girl he wanted to spend the rest of his life with. He'd been wrong.

His blood pounded through his veins at the very thought of them making love again. It was what he'd wanted from her from the first moment he'd set eyes on her in the restaurant. Not that he'd forgiven her for her past actions, or ever would—but it might give him a feeling of satisfaction to use that beautiful body again. Bend her to his will, make her dependent on him, and then maybe… He smiled at the idea entering his mind.

Cade had been devastated when she'd let him down. He'd believed that she'd had more integrity than to plot with her father against him, and his faith in humanity had been badly dented.

Cade's trip out here had nothing to do with Simone. He knew the Whitsundays well, and had simply seen them as the perfect place to set up another branch of his business. He hadn't even known whether Simone still lived in the area. And yet here she was, as vividly beautiful as he remembered— more so, in fact. She was devastatingly, heart-stoppingly stunning with her shiny dark-auburn hair tied back in a cute ponytail, revealing in all its exquisite detail her heart-shaped face and huge, luminous violet eyes. Her mouth was soft and tempting even in the midst of her resentful anger.

He wanted to touch, he wanted to take, and he was not unaware of the effect he'd had on her. She ought to be uncomfortable after what she'd done to him, indeed she'd do well to be afraid of him, But he'd observed her deepened breathing, seen the darkening of her eyes and he guessed that she too was remembering the exciting times they'd spent together.

He'd bet his life that she was wondering what it would be like to be made-love to by him again.

He rigidly pushed such unworthy thoughts to the back of his mind. 'It's not a matter of why I'd help you,' he said tersely. 'It's—how shall I put it?—a matter of expediency. Like I said, I'm looking to expand my business, and picking up the bones of an old one might be better than starting out afresh. I've been looking around; there aren't too many new opportunities here. The area's pretty well covered.'

'You mean you want to take me over?' Simone's eyes widened even further and her chin jutted, lengthening her already long, slender neck.

She looked so beautiful when she was angry. Her cheeks coloured delicately, her eyes flared, and her whole body took on a new, exciting life. It was all he could do not to reach out and touch her, kiss her, feel her against him.

Begin his campaign—take what he wanted and then...

'Not in the least.' Cade sounded normal. How could that be when his heart had begun racing at the mere thought of what he intended to do? 'Think about what I've said, Simone, and we'll meet for dinner tomorrow evening to discuss it.'

Simone struggled with reason. Cade was walking all over her. The point was, did she go along with his suggestion to help her out, or simply admit defeat and fade into nothingness? What exactly did the business mean to her?

Her father was way beyond giving advice; he'd sunk into the misery of a gambler gone beyond his means. He'd added drink to his troubles, and her worried mother, whose heart and health were failing, was now in a nursing home completely unaware of Simone's troubles. Simone still lived with her father, she couldn't afford not to, but apart from cooking him the odd meal they lived independent lives.

So the answer to Cade's question was simple, really—the business meant everything to her. She loved what she was doing. She loved boats, and water and sun and sailing, and the whole way of life. She didn't want to let it go. She didn't owe her father anything—quite the opposite!—but she owed it to her mother to keep the company going. And if what Cade was looking for was an investment—not a takeover—then maybe she ought to consider his offer.

'That's a yes, then?'

Simone hadn't realised Cade had been watching her every expression, that he'd seen the fight she'd had with herself and the conclusion she'd drawn. She nodded, not altogether sure she would be doing the right thing, glancing at him only briefly—because to look straight into his eyes sent vibrations through her body, procreating a hunger she had never imagined possible to feel again.

But perhaps she ought to have looked at him. One moment she was worrying whether she was doing the right thing, the next his mouth had closed on hers in a searing kiss and she was elevated into a world of senses that she had believed was lost to her for ever.

One warm, firm hand cupped either side of her face; his lips demanded and took, and without even realising what she was doing Simone returned his kiss. It was an instinctive response, a throwback to the days of their young, heady relationship. Although common sense told her that she ought to snatch away, something inside insisted she prolong this magical moment.

It might be the last time he ever kissed her. Perhaps it was simply a sealing of their bargain, nothing more. She was aware that it meant nothing, but it was also something beautiful which she wanted to cherish.

Seconds later Cade stepped backwards. 'Good,' he said briskly. 'I'm glad you've seen sense. I'll pick you up at seven tomorrow. You're still living at home, I assume?' Simone gave a quick nod, not trusting herself to speak, and slid into her car. It was a moment or two, though, before she found the strength to turn the key and drive away.

CHAPTER TWO

CADE rang Simone's doorbell at seven precisely. It was almost as though he'd been standing outside looking at his watch, ready to announce his presence at precisely the right second, she thought.

Fortunately, her father was out; she had no idea where and didn't much care. It was not the thought of a loving daughter, she knew, and although Simone knew she would never turn her back on him, Matthew Maxwell had long since lost her respect.

What was uppermost in her mind at the moment were her feelings for Cade. They had returned with such a vengeance when he had kissed her that she was afraid of them, and if she had known how to get in touch with him she would have cancelled their dinner date. It had been incredibly stupid of her to agree in the first place. She had been borne along by the thought of her precious business being saved.

But by Cade?

She had seen the way his eyes narrowed as he'd made a study of her body, and she had caught the tensing of a muscle in his jaw as he'd tried to hide whatever it was he was feeling. And then the kiss! A kiss that could lead nowhere. What had he made of her response?

Could she possibly work with a man who set her body

alight so completely? Who turned her from a normally composed and competent woman into a nervous wreck? Even now, as she moved to open the door, her heartrate was climbing.

She had dressed carefully and conservatively. She wanted to give him no wrong ideas. She wore a pastel-pink long skirt and a matching top with a demure V-neckline and short sleeves. She teamed it with high-heeled sandals and wore mother-of-pearl earrings that reflected the pink of her outfit.

Her hair was fastened up in a neat twist, and her mirror had told her that she looked cool and calm and in full control of her emotions. Stupid mirror! She was a mess inside, crammed with teeming sensations that threatened to spill over and tell the real story.

Nevertheless when she opened the door she kept her chin firm and wore a faint smile. And then she nearly staggered backwards as the full breadth of Cade's sexuality impacted on her senses.

She'd spent all of the previous night dreaming about him—dreams she preferred not to recall. Then had spent all day psyching herself up so that she could present an indifferent front—but one look into his staggeringly handsome face and every good intention had flown off into space, never to be recovered.

'Aren't you going to invite me in?' he asked, when she stood there clutching the door.

Was he aware that if she let it go she would fall down? Simone smiled faintly and tested her reaction. Actually, no, she wouldn't fall. She was still capable of standing—just about. She stepped back and let Cade enter. But instead of walking straight past her he stopped, and for one earth-shattering moment she thought he was going to kiss her again. Simone prepared herself to flee, but all he did was touch a kiss to his fingertips before pressing them to her brow.

'I don't bite, Simone. You needn't look so scared.'

'Is that what you think, that I'm afraid of you?' she asked, trying to ignore the pain in her forehead where he had just branded her. 'What I am concerned about is that you should have had a wasted journey.'

Golden eyes suddenly narrowed, his head tilted to one side. 'Because?'

Simone didn't know what had prompted her to make that statement. Self-defence, probably. She eyed him coldly. 'Your idea. You know it won't work, Cade, the two of us together. We have too much history.'

His eyes closed even further, until it looked as though he was squinting into the sun. But instead of feeling menaced Simone experienced a dramatic stampede of her senses. Without a doubt if she went through with this merger with Cade she would end up more of a wreck than she already was.

'So what are you saying?' he wanted to know. 'That I'm wasting my time?'

'Precisely that,' she agreed, catching a sharp breath. 'I think—'

'And I think that you cannot do without me,' he cut in brutally. 'We'll talk here, if you like. Are your parents home?'

Simone shook her head. At least Cade didn't know the full extent of her personal problems. Apart from her father's business dealings, his hedonistic lifestyle had almost ruined her mother's life too. Unable to cope with her husband's increased absences from home, Simone's mother had become depressed, and in her weakened state had suffered a near-fatal heart attack that had left her so fragile she had practically given up on life. She was now in a nursing home, and Simone was desperate to protect her mother as much as she could.

'Then I'll order in.'

'No!' declared Simone in blind panic. There would be no escape then, she would be trapped by her raging emotions. Already they were threatening to run out of control. Cade was a force to be reckoned with. Without even trying, he had turned her into an emotional mess. And entertaining him here would add to her torment.

'I guess I'm not easy in your presence,' she admitted eventually. 'So much water has gone under the bridge.'

'Or maybe it's because you have a guilty conscience.'

Simone saw a flash in his eyes, quickly controlled, but it was a warning all the same. He could be as nice to her as he liked, but beneath his charming veneer was a wolf ready to pounce.

He didn't wait for an answer. 'We'll carry on as planned, and you can tell me everything that's been going on in your life. Why your business is tumbling downhill at a faster rate than an avalanche in the Alps, or what happened to the money you and your father tricked me out of, for instance,' he suggested, his mouth grim all of a sudden.

At Cade's mention of the past, and the reason they had split all those years ago, Simone knew she had no choice but to agree to Cade's request, if only to explain once and for all. She also knew that despite their bitter and complicated past Cade was her last chance of saving her company. However, the thought of dining out with the sexiest man on the planet did her no good at all. By the end of an evening spent trying to hide her churning emotions, she would be a gibbering wreck.

When she discovered that he had hired a chauffeur-driven Mercedes, compelling her to sit cosily in the back with him, she felt even more anti-Cade. Memories returned of her eighteenth birthday when he had hired just such a car. They'd virtually made love on the back seat, the driver politely averting his eyes as they'd almost eaten each other alive.

It crucified her to think how easily she had given herself to him. She'd been so eager, it must have been embarrassing. No, that was wrong. Cade hadn't been embarrassed in those days; she had excited him.

Despite the inches that separated them she could feel him as fiercely as if their bodies were touching. His cologne invaded her nostrils, intoxicating and arousing, and she suddenly found she wanted to experience his arms about her once more. She wanted his kisses, she wanted…

Deliberately Simone closed her mind to such thoughts. She wanted nothing. Tonight without a doubt was going to be a total disaster. It would be impossible to spend several hours in his company without giving herself away. He tortured her soul simply by being there. His very presence was consuming, making her head spin and her mind shift out of kilter.

And they were supposed to be making some sort of business deal!

Was she crazy or what? It would never work. It was a recipe for disaster.

It was a relief when the car pulled up in front of a new hotel in Airlie Beach. It had been open for only a few months, and was massively impressive—and very, very expensive.

Cade led her to a lift, swiping his security pass, giving her scarcely any time to look about her. It shot smoothly upwards, but it wasn't until the doors opened that Simone realised they were in the penthouse suite. She looked at him in alarm.

'What's going on?' Her heartrate tripled in a matter of seconds.

Any time spent alone with Cade was dangerous, but this threatened to go right off the Richter scale.

'I thought we'd dine in my suite,' he answered, his smile

devilishly disturbing. 'It's far more private and will give us the opportunity to talk.'

'There's nothing we have to say that's so very private,' insisted Simone, panic beginning to set it. 'And if you think that I'm up for anything else then you're very much mistaken.'

But Simone realised that the biggest mistake of all had been in agreeing to dine out with him in the first place. Cade had changed. He was no longer the exciting lover who had tenderly led her into the pleasures of love-making. He was a dangerous man on a mission—and the trouble was she didn't know what he had in mind.

Cade was being driven crazy by Simone's sweetly scented body. After that kiss, all too brief though it was, he'd known that she too felt a reincarnation of the animal hunger they'd once indulged. Oh yes, she was denying it, but why bring the subject up if she wasn't experiencing a resurrection of old feelings?

He was strongly tempted to follow his instincts and touch her, stroke her smooth, sensitive skin that smelled so enchanting, kiss her beautiful soft mouth again, make her totally his. Would she oppose him, he wondered? Or would she let her emotions fly free and use her voluptuous body to weave its magic the way it had always done?

The very thought sent his male hormones into painful orbit, and he had to use all his resources to compose himself. When the lift doors had opened Simone had been the first to step out into the carpeted foyer with its elegant mirrored walls. Her stride was long, her back straight, her whole demeanour haughtily beautiful.

She walked straight through into the hugely spacious living area, with its floor-to-ceiling windows and stunning views over the deep turquoise-blue of the Pacific. When she turned to face him, her expression was a mixture of defiance and curiosity.

'Your business must be hugely successful, if you can afford to stay in a place like this.'

'It's doing OK,' he answered.

Her fine brows rose, widening her already huge, expressive eyes. He used to feel that he could drown in them. Cade shook his head. It was far too poetical a thought for a tough businessman, he decided now. Nevertheless they brought back memories that were seriously disturbing.

She still had the most tempting body of any women he knew. She'd not gained an ounce of weight, and was so slender that she looked as though a light breeze would blow her away. Her rounded breasts pushed tantalisingly against the soft fabric of her top, and he could picture them free of any encumbrance.

Damn, he wasn't supposed to be thinking like this. Not yet, at any rate. This was a business meeting. If he wasn't careful he'd frighten her away before he'd even started. The main reason for his return visit to Australia was to explore the possibilities of setting up a new branch. He'd been excited at the thought, it had incubated in his mind for a long time, and when he'd discovered that there were no opportunities exactly where he'd wanted them frustration had got the better of him.

Enter Simone!

Killing two birds with one stone had instantly seemed like a good idea to him. Nevertheless, he knew he mustn't rush. If his plan was going to be successful then he must gain her total trust first—except that pushing to one side the host of frenetic desires that had burst into life inside his body was not going to be easy.

Cade had always prided himself on his ability to control

his feelings. But he hadn't counted on the impact Simone Maxwell would still have on him. For years he had told himself that he hated her. She had pulled the worst trick imaginable, and for that he would never forgive her.

But her body was a different story altogether. It was sensational, tantalising in the extreme. A man would have to be inhuman not to be affected. She wore nothing provocative today, but in covering up she had made herself more of a target. She was all woman—she could wear sackcloth and not be any sexier—and he was all virile male. A striking combination!

When the two got together worlds would explode. He smiled. It was an image worth hanging on to.

His thoughts were disturbed by a silent-footed waiter wheeling in a heated trolley bearing their meal, and he then proceeded to open the bottle of champagne already nestling in ice.

Cade observed Simone watching the man's deft movements as he filled two glasses, and wondered exactly what was going through her mind. Her face was a mask of controlled feelings. She looked calm and beautiful, but he knew that inside she was seething. She did not want to be here, she'd made that very clear, and he knew that she would try and use any excuse to make a swift exit.

He dismissed the man, telling him softly that he did not wish to be disturbed again, and then handed Simone her champagne flute. 'Come and sit down. I promise I won't bite,' he said, and soft music began to play in the background.

'I can't promise that *I* won't bite,' Simone retorted, her eyes flashing a fiery purple. Instead of sitting, she walked over to the window. The sky was darkening; soon there would be nothing to see. And then she would have no choice but to devote all of her attention to him.

Simone wondered what she had let herself in for. Dining

with Cade had been one thing, but spending time in his luxurious suite was another. Had she walked into a trap? Was discussing a business deal the last thing on his mind? Was she right to question his motives?

All these thoughts and more rushed like a maelstrom through her mind. To be honest, her own hormones were raging; why wouldn't they be when faced with a man so blatantly sexy as Cade Dupont? But she was controlling them. She felt sure that he hadn't a clue how she felt. Yet at the same time she was very much aware that he wanted more from her than a simple business arrangement.

When she felt his warm breath on the back of her neck Simone knew that she was right to be worried. But amazingly all he did was touch a firm hand to her arm and lead her over to one of the leather sofas in the centre of the room. *All he did!* His touch was like a branding iron, and she couldn't wait for him to let go.

'You seem a little—on edge,' he said once they were comfortable. 'Why is that?'

Damn the man! He knew what was wrong. She certainly wasn't going to spell it out to him. 'I'm overwhelmed,' she answered instead, and took a sip of champagne. It tasted good, but she promised herself no more, because she needed to keep a clear head. She set the glass down on the low table at her side.

'This place is new, I understand,' he said.

'And it costs a fortune to stay here,' she returned. 'They've had royalty and film stars, but it's certainly not in my league.'

'Do you know?' he said softly, too softly, 'I really thought you'd have been a very rich woman by now. What happened, Simone?'

Simone drew in a deep breath and stared him in the eye. Why not? He'd badger her anyway until she told him, so she might as well get it over with. 'My father gambled away everything,' she confessed with a defensive tilt to her chin. 'He's now drinking himself slowly to death.' She hated having to tell this man what a sorry figure her father had become, but if he was going to help then she had to be totally honest.

Cade's lips suddenly tightened. 'So that's where my money went.' His nostrils dilated as he took a deep breath. 'I wish to God I'd never met you, Simone Maxwell,' he said, his voice thick with emotion. 'I had no idea you were a woman of such low principles. You made a fool of me all those years ago. Damn it, you deserve to be—'

'Stop it!' Simone's eyes shot sparks of purple anger. 'Cade, like I said at the time, I didn't know what my father was up to. He fooled me exactly the same as he fooled you!'

'And I'm supposed to believe that?' Cade snorted. 'I know what you want me to believe, Simone, and why, but he told me. He explained that you were in on it together, so please don't lie to me any more.'

Simone stiffened. She couldn't believe what she was hearing. 'If that's what he said, then he was the one lying,' she protested, horrified to think that her father had shifted part of the blame on to her. 'I asked you to invest in all innocence, Cade. I thought it would be good for you…for us.'

Cade's eyes flashed his disbelief. 'I'd be a fool to believe that now. I paid dearly for what you did to me, Simone.'

'And you think I haven't suffered?' she cut in frostily. 'I've suffered plenty. My mother's in a home because of my father's behaviour. I'm about to lose my business. I have a—' She pulled herself up short. Perhaps this was not the right time to tell Cade about her failed marriage. 'And my father—well, he's not my father any more. Not the man I knew. My life's hell, if you must know.'

She got up and walked over to the window again. There was something calming about watching the ocean, and she desperately needed calm at this moment. Her breathing was all over the place and she wanted to throw something—preferably at Cade Dupont's handsome face. She drew in a deep breath and held it, then let it go again. Twice more she did this, closing her eyes now, letting her thoughts drift back to that fateful time nearly five years ago.

She had been going out with Cade for almost fifteen months when he had announced out of the blue that he had inherited a considerable sum of money from his paternal grandfather. 'What are you going to do with it?' she had asked, hoping that maybe he would propose to her, and that they would buy a lovely house to live in.

'I'm going into business,' he had announced.

Simone had hid her disappointment, but had shown a genuine interest in Cade's dream. 'What sort of business?'

'I don't know yet,' he had answered. 'I need to give it some thought.'

When she had told her father, he had immediately wondered whether Cade would like to buy into a new boat-building company he was considering setting up. 'I've been thinking about it for some time,' he had said. 'I was looking for an investor, and Cade might be the perfect person. It will go hand in hand very nicely with our current business. How about you ask him if he'd be interested?'

So Simone had put the idea to Cade, telling him what a good investment it would be, hoping that it would unite their families and make a future proposal from Cade a certainty. Cade had been interested, and, after much consideration and consultation with her father, he'd decided to take Matthew Maxwell up on his offer. Neither of them had known, especially not Simone, that her father had had no intention of setting up another business. What he had been after was simply more money to cover his gambling debts.

It had only been afterwards, when Cade had discovered that he'd lost all his money, that Simone had realised what her father was up to. She had never forgiven him. And now Cade hadn't forgiven her either. He was firmly convinced that she'd been in on the con trick and he wouldn't listen to anything she had to say.

He had flown to England very shortly afterwards. It was where Cade had been born and had lived until he was twelve. Simone had been heartbroken, and even more so when he hadn't returned her phone calls. Her mobile phone had been red-hot for weeks, sending texts and messages to his voice mail. But he'd ignored every one of them. And as the months had turned into years she had accepted the fact that she would never see Cade again.

And now he was here, larger than life and just as overwhelming.

Without warning his arms snaked around her waist, and she was pulled back against the hard, exciting length of him. She didn't fight. What was the point? Fighting Cade had always been useless. And, actually, it felt good to be held by him. She dropped her head back on his shoulder, felt his warm breath feathering her cheek, and for one crazy moment she wished that things were different between them.

But they weren't, and they never would be. 'I'm sorry things haven't worked out for you,' he said, his voice surprisingly soft.

Simone remained silent. He was saying what he thought she wanted to hear. He didn't mean it. Too much had happened between them for him to be genuine. He was only offering to help with the business because it would be to his benefit. Cade would probably tie her up in complicated legal knots, and she'd sign her life away and be left with nothing. *Just as he thought she had done to him!*

As this second thought struck her, Simone struggled to free herself. Cade was clever, but not clever enough. 'Don't worry about me, Cade, I'm all right,' she insisted.

'Then I suggest we begin our meal.' He sounded incredibly satisfied as he led her to the table, confirming in Simone's mind that she had every reason to be wary of him. It didn't stop her responding to his sex appeal, though. It was so strong that it came across her in waves of thick emotion. She had only to breathe the air around them to feel an instant stirring of her senses.

He was so insufferably arrogant these days that she didn't know how she could possibly react so wildly. It had to be a throwback to her youth, and the heady rush she had felt as she had fallen in love for the first time. It was said that no one ever forgot their first love. Well, she most certainly had never forgotten Cade. What she hadn't expected was for the same feelings to come tumbling back.

She found herself hungering for his kisses, wondering whether they would be the same as they had been or whether he'd improved. She used to think that was impossible; how could you improve on perfection? But where Cade was concerned she was quickly beginning to learn that anything was feasible.

In the centre of the table was a red rose in a bud vase. Simone hadn't noticed it before, and she winced as she remembered that this was Cade's signature tune before spending a romantic evening together.

She felt like picking the vase up and flinging it across the room, but of course she didn't. She ignored it, sitting perfectly still instead.

'You've gone very quiet all of a sudden,' said Cade as he filled their wine glasses. 'What are you thinking?'

His voice, deep and amused, had her looking up with a startled expression in her lovely eyes. 'Nothing,' she answered.

'Impossible. Unless, of course, by nothing you mean that I was the object of your thoughts, mmm?'

Of course he knew that she'd been thinking about him. He'd always had an invisible antenna that picked up on her thoughts whenever he was in them. It looked like some things never changed, and that she'd need to be even more wary in future.

'It would be pretty ridiculous not to think about you when you're right here in front of me,' she replied sharply.

Cade raised his glass. 'Here's to us, then. To a successful partnership.'

Simone eyed him warily. 'Partnership?' She wasn't aware that she had agreed to anything yet.

'What else would you call it?'

'Nothing,' she said quickly, trying to dismiss the fact that she'd been thinking he might want a complete takeover. 'To our partnership,' she agreed reluctantly, lifting her glass too, knowing she had absolutely no other choice.

'And to the future,' he said. 'Whatever that might hold.'

There was silence for a few seconds, each deep in their own thoughts, and then Cade smiled and said, 'I've ordered oysters for our entrée, Simone. Kilpatrick, just as you like them.'

He remembered. But oysters? Oysters and champagne— both aphrodisiacs, allegedly! Was that what this evening was all about? Did he want to get her into his bed?

The very thought sent serious sensations zinging their way through her. She tightened the muscles at the apex of her thighs, and vowed not to let herself give way to temptation. The trouble was he was still so utterly, utterly gorgeous. Long, dark lashes framed his amazing golden eyes, his nose was straight and only slightly flared, and his mouth—not too generous, not too small— Well, she ached to be kissed by those exciting lips.

'Of course, there'd be interest to pay.' He was back to the main topic of conversation.

Faint alarm had her looking sharply at him. 'Even though you'd be a partner?'

'Even so.' He pushed himself up and walked ever so slowly round the table towards her, his eyes on hers every inch of the way, never deviating, never blinking.

Simone's heartbeats increased to a treacherous level. She had a feeling she wasn't going to like what he had to say next. He wasn't talking about money here, it was something far more dangerous.

'So what is it exactly you want from me, Cade?' she asked when he came to a halt at her side. She could feel the heat of his skin, see the dark pupil in the centre of his eyes, smell the dangerous male scent of him. Every one of her senses was on high alert.

'I'll turn your company around in return for…'

Simone knew what he was doing. He was testing her nerves, wanting to see whether she'd back out before he put any clauses into their agreement. She stood up and looked straight into his face, trying not to show the panic swirling inside her.

His golden eyes blazed into hers, claiming her, making her his before he'd even spoken. 'In return for you in bed beside me. Every night. As my mistress. No concessions. If you want to keep your business, you've no choice.'

CHAPTER THREE

CADE watched Simone's changing emotions. Her outrage at his suggestion that she become his mistress was exactly what he'd expected. She would come round, though. He was prepared to bet his last dollar on it. She'd made it perfectly clear that she didn't want to lose her company.

In theory he already part-owned it.

His lips thinned as he recalled that fateful day when he'd signed his inheritance away. Despite her protestations, Simone had been involved in that and he wanted to take hold of her and shake her until she begged for mercy. Then he smiled to himself. Making her his mistress would definitely be a more pleasurable way of punishing her than anything else he could think up.

She'd already sent out enough signals to show her interest, and he knew that she was going to agree to his request. It was simply a matter of fighting her conscience. It amused him to watch the conflicting emotions cross her face.

'Surely you must know I can't do it?' she asked, her deeply violet eyes sparking with indignation, her whole body rejecting his suggestion. 'I cannot possibly prostitute myself like that.'

Cade struggled to control lips desperately trying to smile. She looked beautiful in her anger, so much so that he wanted to kiss her. In fact, he wanted to take her to bed right now. 'From where I'm standing you don't have much choice,' he said, his heart leaping at the thought of the pleasure that would stem from such a liaison.

'Everyone has a choice,' she told him heatedly. 'I don't have to do anything I don't want to do.'

'So you'd rather lose your company?' He moved a few inches closer. 'The choice is yours, Simone. But if you do agree then the repayment will be as I have outlined. What you and your father did to me was unpardonable, Simone. If I help you, then you owe me big time.'

'My father—'

He didn't allow her to finish. His eyes hardened. 'Forget the excuses. They won't wash, and I'm tired of hearing them.' Anger surfaced as memories returned.

'So you want my body instead?' she snapped.

'I'm simply eliciting a long-overdue payment,' he answered tersely. 'And, if you care as much about MM Charters as you profess, you really have no other option.'

Exactly, thought Simone. But she sure as hell wasn't going to let him walk all over her. She was no pussycat; this cat had claws, and she would use them if necessary. However she felt about Cade, the thought of becoming his mistress was both exhilarating and devastating at the same time. It would be the ultimate humiliation for her—but would the saving of her company more than make up for it?

'I'll need to think about it,' she said quietly.

But Cade shook his head. He had no intention of letting her go that easily. When he'd seen her in the restaurant it had set off a chain of emotions, and he'd known there and then that he had to have her one more time. Treading gently wasn't part of his make-up, and if he wanted something he went all out to get it. He'd applied that principle in every aspect of his life, both business and personal, and he wasn't about to change. 'I'm sorry, Simone, but I need an answer now or the offer's withdrawn,' he told her none too gently.

He enjoyed watching the battle she had with herself. She turned away from him and crossed towards the window, folding her arms and staring out blindly into the night.

'Perhaps,' he said quietly, following her, 'I should give you a taste of what you'll be missing should you turn down my offer.' And without even waiting for a response he twisted her round into his arms. He felt her limbs go taut and he knew that she would hate every moment. Nevertheless he snaked a hand round the back of her neck and lowered his face to hers.

When their lips met sensations flew in all directions. His body flooded with red-hot desire. He kissed her deep and hard, running his tongue inside her mouth, tasting the sweetness of her, feeling her involuntary response.

Fire raged in his chest, in his loins, and he wanted her so badly that it hurt. She smelled so heavenly, tasted so good, that he didn't want to let her go.

If this was an indication of things to come, should Simone agree to his conditions, then the whole experience would be well worth the cost. He'd be getting the business he wanted and the sweetest of revenges into the bargain.

Simone's heart drummed unsteadily. It felt like a live thing in her breast, hollering to be let out. Panic stations had set in when Cade had kissed her, and despite lecturing herself on the stupidity of returning his kiss she'd been unable to help herself. It had been an instinctive response to a man who could liquefy her bones with one glance. A man who could turn her world upside down without even speaking.

One touch and she was putty in his hands. One dark glance

out of those devilishly golden eyes and she was his. She hated herself for being weak, but in truth she wanted his kisses; she wanted him to make love to her.

He created excitement such as she had never experienced before. Not even when they'd been going out together. Everything had intensified. But to barter her body for a business deal—could she even consider doing such a thing? Her answer was a resounding yes. MM Charters meant everything to Simone, and she had to be honest and admit that it wasn't as though she wouldn't enjoy sleeping with Cade. It would be mind-blowing, like it always had been between them. But it was the afterwards that bothered her. How would she feel then, when it was all over? When Cade had finished using her and had discarded her—would she be able to walk away too?

She dared not think along those lines. She had felt dead inside for months after he'd gone last time. She had to think of this moment, of the trouble she was in now, and Cade's offer of help.

Simone drew in a deep breath, closed her eyes and then snapped them open, finding herself looking into a barrier of intense gold. 'I'll do it,' she said quickly before she could change her mind.

His response was to kiss her again. She felt the hot strength of his body against hers, the throbbing of his heart almost in unison with her own, and the urgent need that rose inside her. It almost made her ashamed of herself. She was selling her body—and yet kissing Cade felt so right. It always had done. Their sex life had been incredible. He had taught her so much.

The kiss was fierce but short. She was disappointed when Cade took her shoulders and put her from him. 'Good, I'm glad that's settled,' he said matter-of-factly. 'Let's start our dinner.'

Humiliation filled Simone, hot and strong. Stark realisation hit hard in her chest. This was nothing more than a business deal to Cade, whereas she had stupidly felt a stirring of old emotions. He was going to take her body whenever he felt like it, but there would be no love involved, no tenderness. It was as simple as that.

They ate their meal in silence, Simone simply picking at the oysters and the excellent barramundi that followed, shaking her head when Cade suggested dessert.

'Do you remember the Valentine's Ball?'

His question took her by surprise. How could she not remember? It had been the first time Cade had taken her out, and she had worn a beautiful off-the-shoulder dress in emerald satin. He had told her that she looked a million dollars, and she had glowed beneath his compliment.

When he'd seen her home at the end of the evening she had felt as though she was walking on air. And after that their romance had blossomed sensationally.

'I will remember it for ever,' she answered, unaware how wistful her voice had gone.

'You were stunning even then.' His eyes made a study of her face, watching every fleeting expression, resting for several long seconds on the soft contours of her mouth.

Hiding her reaction was a sheer impossibility, thought Simone, as she touched a nervous tongue to lips that had gone dry. And when those same gorgeous eyes visited each part of her body in turn she felt an even more dramatic arousal of feelings.

She had no idea that her breathing had deepened, that her breasts were rising and falling a little faster than usual. Or that Cade had observed this tiny detail. 'Maybe we should drink our coffee somewhere more comfortable,' he suggested.

But not sit together, decided Simone, choosing an easy chair rather than one of the sofas. Lamps in the beautifully appointed apartment bathed the whole room in softly seductive light. At any other time…

Cade fixed himself a drink at the bar, and Simone was pleased at the temporary respite from his presence. Nevertheless she couldn't take her eyes off him. She watched every movement he made. His clothes both hid and revealed a body that was in great shape. One that had once belonged intimately to her.

He was the one man she had truly loved—and then lost for ever.

'Are you sure you don't want one?' He looked up and smiled, and her heart did a flip.

'I'm sure,' she answered, her voice kitten-soft.

When he returned to his seat she avoided looking at him. He was seriously sexy and out to charm her again—but for no reason other than she was part of his business plan. She must remember that.

Everything inside her had sprung into life, until she felt as though she was wired to a machine that kept shooting electrical impulses through her veins. She wished he had never come back. She'd had her heart broken once by him, and if a heart could be broken a second time then Cade was the man to do it.

Long minutes ticked by when neither of them spoke. Cade watched Simone through half-closed eyes, a faint smile on his lips, arousing her without the need for words. This was an old game between them, and one they had played many times before. Simone thought back to how it had usually played out. When she had taken so much that her insides had begun to sizzle. She used to respond to Cade's silent arousals by stripping her clothes off in a slow, seductive dance. Then she'd begin to unrobe him as well—except usually by that time he'd been too impatient and had torn his clothes off himself.

But if he thought his tactics would work now he was deeply

mistaken. OK, she'd agreed to become his mistress, but she wasn't giving him her body quite so easily this time around.

Then Cade broke the spell by speaking on a totally different subject. 'I actually expected you to be married by now.'

Simone drew in a deep breath, pulling a wry face as she did so. She might as well tell him the truth; he would find out anyway. 'I was married, actually. I'm divorced.' She added bitterly, 'It's another part of my life that ended in disaster.'

Dark brows rose, and there was a long pause when she could see his mind working overtime before he asked, 'What happened?'

'He walked out on me,' she answered tersely. 'He met someone else.' It was all she was prepared to tell him at this stage.

'I'm sorry,' he said, and oddly enough he sounded as though he meant it. 'And there's no one else who might be upset if he knew I was entertaining you here? If he knew the position you're now in?'

'Would I have agreed if there was?' snapped Simone.

Cade smiled exultantly.

Simone felt like slapping him. Instead she shot a retaliatory question. 'Have you ever married?' There was no ring on his finger, but that didn't mean a thing.

He shook his head. 'I've had no time. Girlfriends, yes, but marriage has definitely been off my agenda.'

Simone was surprised. If he could afford to bail her out, throw in as much as it needed to buy a new fleet of sailing vessels without even batting an eyelid, then he had to be seriously rich. And seriously rich men attracted girls by the dozen. So why hadn't one of them captured his heart?

'Or is it that you've set yourself impossibly high standards?' she asked without thinking, and Cade's harsh response surprised her.

'When someone lets you down badly it does make you think twice,' he snarled, his eyes cutting through hers like twin blades of ice. 'Trust has to be earned, and no one yet has earned enough merit points.'

It felt like a direct dig, at her and Simone silently winced. Nevertheless she raised her chin and looked at him boldly. 'Merit points? How calculating. Exactly what are you looking for in a wife, Cade? No one's perfect.'

'As I discovered for myself, most brutally. Maybe there's a halfway mark somewhere.'

His eyes darkened as he looked at her. Simone felt a trickle of something slide down her spine. Was it fear or hope? Need she be afraid of him? He was going to help her. That had to be good. But the cost was exorbitantly high, and she couldn't help wondering whether it would be worth it.

Feeling a desperate need to change the subject, she said, 'Exactly what is it you propose to do—as far as my company's concerned?'

Cade set his glass down and changed instantly into business mode. 'I've drawn up a rough plan of action— provided you agree, of course.' But his dangerous eyes told her that she had no option.

'Naturally the first thing would be a whole new fleet of boats, which I've already looked into ordering. Then your offices would need to be totally revamped, everything brought bang up to date.'

Simone widened her eyes. 'Is that necessary?' It was an entirely unexpected suggestion, and she couldn't see his reasoning behind it. What was wrong with her office?

'It's very necessary. A new image will do the business a world of good,' he answered bluntly.

Cade clearly knew what he was talking about, and it was

his money he was spending, so who was she to argue? 'So, tell me about *your* company,' she said finally, not realising that it looked as though she was agreeing to his suggestion.

Cade smiled and settled back into his seat. This was clearly a subject he relished. 'I started with one boat, specialising in corporate charter, and was amazed how quickly it took off. Of course, the season's shorter in the UK, but I did very well. I ended up buying more vessels even after one season.'

'I'm pleased for you,' she said, and surprised herself by meaning it. Cade had exactly the right outlook on life to succeed in whatever he did, and she felt sure that her father's trickery had helped make him into the tough businessman he was today.

'How big is your fleet?'

'To be honest, I'm not sure,' came his staggering answer. 'I've expanded into Europe, so the company is growing at an incredible rate.'

Simone raised her brows. 'So much so soon!' She didn't realise how sour her voice was. 'You must be very good at it,' she conceded. 'I wish my father had had your acumen; I wouldn't be in the trouble I'm in now. Actually, I think he only passed the business on to me because it was failing. Except that he didn't tell me. I was thrilled and so grateful, and now look at the position I'm in.'

'You're forgetting that you have me to bail you out,' he said with a droll smile. 'Your money worries are over.'

He looked calm and reassuring, happy to be of help, and yet she knew perfectly well that beneath the surface lay a cold, calculating brain, and that he was going to walk all over her. She desperately needed his help—he was her lifesaver—but she couldn't rid her mind of the fear that one day she would regret her decision.

'I'd like to go home now,' she said quietly.

'Home?' he repeated, crooking one eyebrow. 'Have you already forgotten we've struck a deal? Your place is here with me.'

Simone hadn't expected him to want his pound of flesh so instantly, and fire flared from her deeply purple eyes. 'Forgive me, but I don't remember setting a date and time for the deal. No job starts immediately.'

'Job?' Distinct amusement curved his mouth and added creases to the corners of his eyes. 'Is that how you see the title of mistress? Interesting! But of course you must go home.'

Instant relief filled Simone, though her reprieve was short-lived.

'You'll need to collect whatever clothes and toiletries you might need—and perhaps tell your father what you're doing.'

'So I'm expected back here this evening?' she questioned, panic in her voice now.

'You have a problem with that? We can of course forget the whole thing. I'll sit by and watch your company sink into the Pacific without trace, and then I'll pick up the threads and establish myself a very profitable concern.' His voice dipped lower and his eyes locked into hers. 'Would you like that, Simone?'

The expression on her face was his answer.

'No, I didn't think so. Excuse me a moment...' He summoned his driver to have the car ready, and when it came she had no choice but to accompany him out of the hotel to the waiting limousine.

She didn't speak for the entire journey, far too conscious that in a few hours' time she would be sharing Cade's bed. It would be the ultimate sacrifice, and would mean that the family business would be safe for ever. She was doing all this for her mother's sake. At least that was what she kept telling herself. It couldn't be that she hungered for Cade's body, could it? No! She wanted to put money back into the bank in the sure knowledge that her father would be unable to touch it. How he would hate that. And how happy she would be.

When they arrived at her house she scrambled out of the car. 'I won't be long,' she promised, and ran up the steps, unaware that Cade had silently followed until he took the key from her hand. 'Allow me.'

'There's no need,' she declared in panic. Was there to be no respite from this man? She had hoped for breathing space before committing herself to him. Instead he wasn't giving her a second's time to herself. Was he afraid that she might change her mind?

He turned the key and pushed open the door, stepping inside before her. The alarm was set and Simone turned it off, accepting the fact that her father was not home. Perhaps that was just as well! She didn't want the two men to meet.

'I find it hard to believe you're still living in this house,' he said with a surprising change of subject, moving further along the hall towards the family room. 'Doesn't it bother you? Where did you live when you were married—not here, surely?'

Simone couldn't see that it was any of his business. She loved this house. It was where she had been born and brought up, and she would always call it home.

'We bought a house,' she told him quietly. 'But I came home when it didn't work out.' And now she hadn't the money to live anywhere else. Her time would come, though; her saviour was right here beside her, a stepping-stone to a better life.

Simone didn't realise that she was staring at Cade until he took a step closer, his eyes on her lips, and she sensed that he was going to kiss her again. She moved quickly. 'I'll go and pack my bags,' she said quickly in a tight, strangled voice.

Cade smiled. He was fully aware that Simone abhorred the

fact she'd been forced to sell her body to him. It proved a number of things, though: that she thought a lot of the charter company and didn't want to see it go under, and also that she would do anything for money. Cade thought back to his treatment at her hands many years ago. After what she'd done, no punishment would be too great.

While waiting for her, he prowled around the downstairs rooms. They were a lot shabbier than they used to be. A lick of paint wouldn't go amiss, he thought. He was surprised that Simone was content to stay here, especially with a happy gambler of a father. He turned his nose up in disgust when he saw evidence of her father's drinking, and instead went in search of Simone, who was taking an inordinately long time to collect her things. He found her sitting on the edge of her bed gazing into space.

'Have you finished?' he asked peremptorily. He didn't particularly want to be here when her father came home; he knew that he'd have some harsh words to say to Matthew Maxwell.

He loathed the man for what he'd done to him, and he held no pity for either him or Simone. She'd known what she was doing all right, and he felt no compunction about using her as a means to an end. It would be a very pleasurable means.

Startled out of her reverie, Simone's beautiful eyes widened. They had always been her most beautiful feature, and he couldn't help thinking that she looked like a trapped deer. In fact she seemed almost afraid of him. 'Nearly,' she managed, springing up and ramming more clothes into her suitcase.

When she struggled to fasten it, he moved towards her. 'Allow me,' He said, and was surprised when she jerked away at the touch of his hand. 'You're still having second thoughts?' he asked roughly.

It didn't feel good when a woman rebuffed him. Especially

Simone. He snapped the fasteners shut and stood the case on the floor. 'If you want to change your mind, Simone…?'

Ignoring his comment, Simone continued collecting her belongings. She gathered up an armful of shoes from her wardrobe and dropped them into a bag. 'Toiletries.' She looked as though she was completely uninterested in what she took, hardly casting a glance as she threw one thing after the other into a separate carrier. 'That's it, I'm ready.'

He picked up the bags and walked in front of her down the stairs. 'Are you leaving a note for your father? Won't he worry about you?'

Simone threw him a caustic glance. 'The only thing my father worries about these days is whether he has enough money to feed his addictions. But you're right.' And she scribbled a note, leaving it on the breakfast bar. Then without a backward glance, with her back ramrod-straight and her head held high, she walked towards the front door.

It opened before she got there and her father appeared, unsteady on his feet as usual, his pale blue eyes widening when he saw Cade. 'You!' he exclaimed, making a stabbing gesture with one finger.

'Mr Maxwell.' Cade acknowledged the older man with a nod of his head.

'What are you doing here?' the man growled, and then he saw Simone's suitcase and other bags and a deep frown gouged his already lined brow. 'What's going on? Are you leaving, Simone?'

She nodded. 'I'm moving in with Cade, Father. He's going to rescue the business.'

It took several seconds for the significance of what she'd said to sink in, then he guffawed loudly. 'Cade Dupont hasn't the brains or the business acumen. You're misguided, girl, if you think he has. With his track record, you'd do best to run a mile.'

'Track record? You have to be joking!' she retorted. 'You were the one who lost all the money. If going along with Cade's suggestion doesn't work, then I've nothing to lose. I've already hit rock bottom, and you should know it. Goodbye, Father.' And she headed out the door.

She heard Cade say something softly to him but she didn't know what, and she didn't much care. Her father was a lost cause these days. She'd stood by him for far too long. It was time now to live her own life.

CHAPTER FOUR

DURING the return journey to Cade's apartment Simone felt faintly guilty for speaking to her father as she had and promised herself that she would still keep her eye on him.

Sensing her unease, Cade took her hand. 'If you'd like me to get help for your father then...'

His unexpected kindness shocked Simone. 'You're already doing enough,' she cut in, pulling her hand away as sensations she would rather not feel but which she knew she would have to get used to snapped into vibrant life. 'He'll survive. But thank you for offering.'

Had he been a different man, had she hated every bone in his body, she couldn't have gone through with his proposition—no matter how much she'd wanted to save MM Charters. Only the knowledge that the short time spent in Cade's bed would be mind-blowingly satisfying had persuaded her she was doing the right thing.

Nevertheless, it still bothered her. In hindsight she ought to have tested him, seen what she could get away with before prostituting herself so freely. But something deep inside her had urged her on, excitement filling every pore of her body. Had she agreed to his demands too easily?

Back at the smart hotel suite she waited with a rapidly

beating heart for Cade to show her which room they would be sharing, and felt both shock and relief when he suggested that she use the one next to his.

'Just for tonight,' he warned with a smile that troubled her. 'You need time to adjust, I realise that. Get a good night's sleep, and then tomorrow—' his unnerving smile widened '—we're moving out of here. I've found us the perfect beach house.'

Simone wanted to ask how, when, why? But she was robbed of speech. All she could do was look at him in open-mouthed astonishment.

'You're surprised?'

'To put it mildly,' she managed, her voice husky. 'Was this before we met up again? Or—?' She couldn't put the rest of her thoughts into words. They were too bizarre by far.

'I don't believe in wasting time,' he announced briskly. 'Is there anything you need before you—retire for the night? A goodnight kiss, perhaps? Tucking up in bed? I could provide all those—and more.'

His eyes told her what the and more entailed. The gold was so intense that it scared her. He was hungry to make love; it was only out of surprising consideration that he was giving her space tonight. She drew in a deep breath, aware that his eyes dropped to her hardened breasts, to her stinging nipples that were responding of their own volition to his intent gaze.

She turned quickly away. 'There's nothing I want. Thank you.'

'Goodnight, then,' he said softly. 'Sweet dreams.' And the door closed.

Damn the man! He knew perfectly well that she wouldn't sleep. Not with the knowledge that he was next door. Not with the knowledge that they would be sharing a bed tomorrow, and the next day, and the next, for however long it took to satisfy his whim.

The bed was deep and the linen luxurious, but she was too conscious of Cade's nearness, too apprehensive about the future and what it might hold, to even close her eyes. Was he managing to sleep? she wondered. Was Cade's conscience clear? She listened hard but could hear no movement, no sound except the distant swish of the ocean.

Finally, sheer exhaustion made her drop off. But it was a fitful sleep, interspersed with dreams of Cade bending her to his will. In her dreams she held nothing back, felt no shame, and she woke finally to feel even more exhausted than when she'd gone to bed.

A tap on the door preceded a freshly showered, fully dressed Cade carrying a tray. Heavens, he looked gorgeous. She couldn't take her eyes off him. He wore a T-shirt and denim jeans that fitted his fantastic bottom like a glove. The man was seriously sexy.

A sudden heat engulfed Simone, and she had to admit that she already wanted him in bed beside her. In truth, becoming his mistress was going to be no hardship at all. She would happily take what was on offer, reap the immediate benefits, and not even think about the future.

Cade had spent the last three hours wondering how soon he could wake Simone. Suggesting she sleep next door to him had been one of the hardest things he'd ever had to do. His whole night had been tortured by thoughts of her tempting body. Three times he'd taken a cold shower, but it had done nothing to stem the excess hormone levels induced just by thinking about her.

'Good morning,' he greeted her with deliberate cheerfulness. 'You slept well, I presume?' He knew for a fact that she wouldn't have lain there the whole night wishing he was in bed beside her. Becoming his mistress was a necessity, not a pleasure, as far as Simone was concerned. The frown on her face proved it. There was no welcoming smile, nothing except sheer irritation.

'What right have you to walk in here?' she challenged abruptly, not bothering to answer his question.

'It's time you were up.' He kept his voice neutral. 'There are things to be done. I presume you still drink tea in the morning?'

Simone nodded.

'Then I'll leave you to get on with it.' Not that he wanted to go, but with her defences so high it would be pointless hanging around. He had hoped for a better reception. She had disappointed him.

'Thank you, Cade.' Her faint voice followed him as he left the room. His lips were grim. He sure as hell wouldn't be pussyfooting around much longer. As soon as they were settled in the beach house, there would be no closing him out. He would demand and he would take, and she would become his mistress in every way possible.

It was a full half-hour before Simone emerged from her room. A pair of white cut-off trousers sat low on her hips, and a lemon crop-top covered her tempting breasts. She wore no make-up and her rich auburn hair hung loose about her shoulders. She looked like the teenager he'd fallen in love with, and Cade's heart turned over. Desire rose and eddied like a swollen stream, and it took every ounce of willpower not to kiss her right there and then.

'I've ordered breakfast,' he said, deliberately making his tone curt. Otherwise he would have swung her up into his arms and carried her straight back to bed

Simone flashed her beautiful eyes. 'I'm not hungry.'

'Then let's go,' he said quickly. 'There's nothing more to keep us here.' As far as he was concerned, the sooner they settled into the beach house the better. This hotel suite was beautifully appointed, he couldn't fault it, but he wanted Simone to see the beach house. Cade liked the great outdoors, and this hotel room and the charged atmosphere inside it was beginning to suffocate him.

'Maybe I will have a slice of toast.'

Cade smiled inwardly. Simone was rattled. She clearly hated what she had to do to rescue her ailing business. Good! She had hurt him too much in the past for him to treat her kindly, and he was going to make her pay for his help. MM Charters would cost a small fortune to bring it bang up to date, and if Simone really thought that he would hand it over to her at the end of the day with no conditions then she was more foolish than he gave her credit for.

Simone was surprised when Cade drove her to a part of the coast that they'd once made their own. A place where it was so secluded that they had been able to make love in the open air without any fear of being disturbed. She hadn't been here since, and wondered why he had brought her here now instead of to the house they were going to live in.

Her heart pounded at the thought that he might want to relive the past—then it stopped when he pulled up at a viewpoint high above the ocean. 'Look down,' he urged.

A house had been built where the land levelled out, the rooms radiating out from a central pool and garden area. It had its own private beach. And a boat ramp. And a boat—a yacht, actually. Simone knew that the boat alone must have cost a small fortune. Was there ever anything more spectacular?

'This is where we'll be staying?' she asked, unaware that

her eyes had gone as wide as a child's who'd just been shown a magic trick.

Cade smiled and nodded.

'I can't believe you were able to rent this place. If I owned it, I'd never want to leave.'

'Let's go and take a closer look,' he said, and she missed his fleeting expression.

Inside the house was as beautiful as the outside. The rooms were spacious and airy with minimal furniture and fantastic views. It was just incredible, thought Simone.

And she was going to be living here with Cade!

So why was she worried? It was surely the answer to all her problems.

'It's fantastic,' she declared, feeling slightly breathless and pushing her worries to one side for the moment.

'It's pretty special,' agreed Cade. 'I was extremely lucky to find it. Do you think you'll be happy here?'

'How could I not be?' she asked.

'You do realise what I want from you?'

She nodded, apprehension creeping in. She wished Cade hadn't brought the subject up—not when she was doing her very best to forget it.

'Then I think we should seal our contract.' Without giving Simone the opportunity to resist, Cade's strong arms folded around her and his head bowed down to hers.

The kiss was torture to Simone's soul. It was sweet and powerful and resurrected so many memories. So many that she returned Cade's kiss with a passion she hardly recognised, pressing her body fiercely against him, feeling an insane urge to recreate the heady excitement they had once experienced.

She forgot for the moment that Cade was coercing her into

this, that becoming his lover was part of a deal and not the real thing. Her head spun off into dizzying space, her breasts peaked and pushed against him, and she became aware of his burgeoning need.

Breathing became difficult; kissing meant everything. She parted her lips and let him explore her mouth. Their tongues touched and tasted and excited, and she felt as though the top was being blown off her head.

It was Cade who called a halt, who gently put her from him. 'That's enough for now.'

Immediately Simone realised what she had done, and anger rose swift and savage within her breast. How could she have succumbed so freely to such insanity? It was mortifying! Cade had made it perfectly clear that he wanted her body, yes, but only in payment. He had no feelings. He was cruel and indifferent, intending only to humiliate her, and take what he wanted when he wanted.

There was one thing only in his favour. The kiss had proven that becoming his mistress and making love with Cade would perhaps be even more exciting than it had been all those years ago.

It wasn't what she wanted, though. She wanted to hate Cade with every fibre of her being. She had thought at one time that she did. In the dark days after Cade had left her, when he'd never returned her calls and when he'd cut her completely out of his life, she had convinced herself of it. So how could her body behave so treacherously now? It didn't make sense.

'We'll have breakfast out here,' he said, leading her to an outside dining area with a wooden-decked floor and a roof, but open on all sides. The most fantastic thing about it, in Simone's opinion, was that it looked out over the ocean. Her offices did exactly the same, but there was the marina and other buildings either side. Here the view was unimpeded: white, wind-rippled sand, and an ocean that looked as though it had been brush-painted in the clearest of blues and purples and turquoises. On the horizon were the hazy outlines of islands, and above them a hot azure sky.

Perfect.

And she was here with a man who had the ability to turn her world upside down. Forget that it was against her will. Forget that she had been pressured into living with him. Simone knew that she had to simply accept what he was offering and enjoy it while she could.

She sat on a white wicker chair in front of a glass-topped table, and from the kitchen Cade produced croissants, ham, cheese and a dish of ready-prepared fresh fruit. A jug of iced juice and a pot of coffee followed.

'You've done all this?' exclaimed Simone in surprise.

Cade shook his head. 'I've inherited a cook-cum-house-keeper. She doesn't live in, but she organised everything for me earlier. She's a treasure, by all accounts.'

Or was it that money talked? wondered Simone. Considering the length of time he'd been over here, he'd worked miracles. She felt irritated that he had so much wealth that he could buy whatever—or whomever—he liked.

The very thought stuck in her throat, and she felt tempted to get up, walk out and tell him he could stick his offer. That she would find some other way to salvage her company.

But common sense prevailed. Simone knew she had exhausted all other avenues when it came to saving her business financially, and she had only to think about their earlier kiss—the way her body had reacted sensationally to his, the way her feelings had spun almost out of control in the space of a few short seconds—to know that she wouldn't find a better offer anywhere.

They were not much more than twenty kilometres away from her father's house, and yet it was like being in a different world. A world where money was of no importance. Comfort was the name of the game.

Yes, she would most definitely be a fool to walk out. Her family home was comfortable, even luxurious by some standards, but this was a different world altogether. This place had several sitting rooms, palatial bedrooms overlooking the ocean, and even a cinema. Cade might only be renting, but it must be costing him a ridiculous amount of money.

Although the food was delicious, she didn't do it justice, drinking mug after mug of coffee instead and religiously keeping her eyes on the view. She knew that if she kept looking at Cade flames would be ignited between them.

She didn't want to feel that. She didn't want a return of the sensational explosion that had erupted between them. She didn't want her body to hunger for Cade's, to beg him for release. She didn't want to belong to him again.

Except that it was too late. She had already pledged herself. She was his.

'A penny for them.'

Simone snapped out of her reverie and glanced across at Cade, who was watching her with a faint smile on his lips.

'Where were you?'

'Wondering what I was doing here,' she answered honestly. And also wondering why a man should have such infinitely kissable lips. Why a man whom she hadn't seen for years should suddenly come back into her life and still have the ability to make her hunger for his kisses.

'I think you know the answer to that,' he said, a frown dragging his well-marked brows together.

His sudden harsh words jolted Simone into tossing her

head. 'I'm simply overwhelmed, Cade. All of this…' She indicated the house and grounds with a sweep of her hand. 'It's as though you're taking great pleasure in emphasising the way you've stepped up in the world.'

'You don't approve? You don't like what I can do?' Golden eyes narrowed and regarded her closely. 'You don't believe in the pleasures of life? Or is it that you're simply jealous—that you're wishing your business had been as successful as mine?'

'It's not that,' she insisted, searching for an excuse, because she didn't want him to know how much he affected her senses. 'It's—' And she picked up on the first thing that came into her mind. 'It's—well—I wish you'd talk your plans for my business over with me, I would like to be consulted.'

Cade appreciated Simone's honesty. Up until now she had meekly accepted that he would be running things. No, perhaps that was wrong—meek wasn't a word he associated with Simone. He had given her no choice. He had steamrollered her into agreeing to let him sort things out. Either that or she'd lose her business altogether. Nevertheless, he was not about to back down.

'Of course I am prepared to discuss things with you, Simone, but I'm afraid you either do things my way or not at all,' he said firmly. 'If you don't like my method, then you know what you can do.' Hell, he hoped she didn't leap up and tell him to get lost. He was the one who would lose then. And losing was not his intention.

'Yes, I know,' she returned, her eyes bright with resentment. 'I can throw the whole thing in your face and go bankrupt instead. I've half a mind to do it. I've decided I don't much like your conditions.'

An eyebrow quirked. 'It's a little late for that, don't you think?' She looked so beautiful when she was fired up and angry. He loved those high spots in her cheeks, the flash in her fascinating eyes, the way her breasts rose and fell so tantalisingly. 'Although I do wonder whether we should put our—er—*agreement* into writing. Let me think, how would I word it? *"I, Simone Maxwell, do hereby declare that I will be Cade Dupont's mistress in return for his financial help. I further declare that there is no time-limit set on this contract"*. Would that cover it, do you think?'

Simone was not sure whether Cade was joking, but even if he wasn't she took his words as an insult. Without even stopping to think about the consequences, she shot up from the table and aimed the flat of her hand at his face.

She ought to have known that he would block her. Instantly her wrist was caught in a vice-like grip, and his face was pushed up close to hers. She could see the clear whites of his eyes and the pure-gold iris, hard and not amused.

'You're in no position to threaten me, Simone,' he declared fiercely through gritted teeth. 'No position at all!' He rose to his feet, and the instant his other hand curled around the back of her head Simone knew what was going to happen. When his mouth captured hers, all the force was knocked from her body.

His kiss was mind-blowingly sensational; it was meant as a reprimand, but instead it aroused every one of her base instincts. She attempted to push him away, but only because she knew he would expect it, not because it was what she wanted.

Memories as swift and vivid as ever swirled in front of her eyes—Cade making love to her, the way she had always given herself to him with complete abandonment, the ecstasy she could never contain.

It had been a whole new world. She had discovered things about her own body that she had never dreamt existed. New experiences. Excitement such as she had never envisaged—

such sensations, such intense feelings. She had felt that she was finally grown up, that she had become a woman, no longer an innocent girl who could only wonder about that thing called love.

She had been devastated when he left, and had felt that she needed to move on with her life, to rid herself of Cade once and for all. She had almost immediately met and married Gerard, a man so different from Cade that she had thought he would be the perfect antidote. They had been happy, but Gerard had never managed to arouse her in the same way that Cade had. Not that their love-making hadn't been exciting, it had. But it had never quite reached the same level, making her wonder if there was anyone else in the whole wide world who could bring her body to such glorious life as Cade Dupont.

Simone no longer fought him; she allowed her body to melt into his. She returned his kisses with a passion he couldn't possibly ignore, wrapping her arms around him, parting her lips in sweet surrender, tasting the exciting maleness of him.

It was all and more than she remembered. Whether it was because they were in a place where they couldn't possibly be disturbed, whether it was just an unfortunate re-run of old desires, or whether these feelings surging like an express train out of control were the real thing, it didn't matter.

What mattered was this exact moment in time. A capsule of time, to be recalled at will, remembered whenever she felt the need. The need now, though, was excruciating. She couldn't remember ever feeling this deep, deep desire. It was more than that. It was an aching, unbearable hunger that had to be assuaged, as though years of agonising need had built up and needed to be fed.

To hell with the consequences. Cade had invited her here for just this purpose, and she was not going to disappoint him.

Not because there was no way out of it, but because it was what she wanted too. More than she had ever thought possible.

She must be weak, she thought, to feel like this whenever he touched her. Nevertheless, it was something she couldn't help. His arms bound her to him, his body pulsed against hers, she spun out into space and felt herself drift helplessly as he kissed every inch of her face, from her hairline to her chin, from the sensitive area behind her ears to the softly throbbing pulse at the base of her throat.

And that was just for starters!

When he felt no resistance, when she clung and moaned and became putty in his arms, Cade lifted her with the ease of an athlete and, still kissing her, still maintaining sensual, sizzling contact, he carried her into the bedroom she already knew he intended they share.

Not that she even thought about that at this moment in time. She was in a daze. She did not care where he took her, all she needed was merciful release from the tempestuous emotions spiralling out of control through her body. There was an ache deep down in her abdomen, an ache in her breasts, an ache in her throat. They all needed blessed relief.

And he was the man to do it.

'Oh, Cade!' The words escaped her parched, dry throat. It was all she could say as she looked at him through eyes blurred by passion.

'"Oh, Cade" what?' he whispered back as he urgently removed her short cotton top.

She was braless beneath—he must have been aware of it all the time they'd been together—and her fingers curled as he dipped his head and took first one and then the other proud, aching nipple into his mouth.

'What are you doing to me?' she gasped as deep, unfathomable excitement swelled in her belly. She caught hold of his head and held him against her, threading her fingers into his hair, tugging, squirming, exhilaration beyond her wildest dreams dancing through her limbs.

She lifted herself, arching her back, urging her breasts even deeper into his expert mouth and tormenting fingers. 'God, I love this!' she cried, without even realising that she had spoken.

'You always were tempting,' he groaned. 'How could I have forgotten the excitement you create?' With a few swift, economical movements he removed the rest of her clothes, his own too, and for a few seconds he stood looking down at her.

Simone amazed herself by not feeling self-conscious, by actually feeling a thrill that he was appreciating her slender limbs and still-firm breasts. He too had the lithe, lean body of someone who worked out on a regular basis, and she hungered for him beside her, inside her, loving her as only he knew how.

Even as the thought entered her head he was there, skin against skin, need answering need, passion feeding passion. He trailed kisses from her mouth to her throat, from her throat to her breasts, and then slowly, achingly, over the flatness of her stomach to the moist heart of her.

Simone arched herself in readiness, heard Cade's deep, guttural groan, and with the speed of both deep-seated hunger and considerable expertise he slid himself inside her. She was transported to a place where nothing mattered except feelings.

Powerful feelings. Such excitement. Such extreme thrills! Wave after wave of death-defying emotions chased through every vein and every artery, sending her heart into shock waves, and her body throbbing and perspiring, wondering how much it could take.

Never had Cade's love-making been this intense. All those years of absence had built into this crescendo of feeling that threatened to spin her out of this world and into the next.

When she could take no more and her body exploded, when feelings were so extreme that she couldn't keep a limb still, she didn't know whether to feel relief or sadness that it was over. And when Cade reached his point of no return as well, when he finally collapsed beside her, his breathing harsh and his body sleeked with sweat, she lay content.

Later she would think about the consequences. For the moment, however, she had never felt more fulfilled.

Cade was the first to speak. 'That was good for you?'

Simone nodded and smiled faintly, ruefully.

'For me too.' He trailed a lazy finger over the flat plane of her belly. 'You're some woman, Simone. I think extracting payment from you is going to be far more pleasurable than I'd ever imagined.'

'Damn you!' Simone rolled swiftly away. 'Why the hell did you have to bring that up?' Just as she'd been feeling comfortable with him. She didn't want her body to be payment, and she wished Cade hadn't put it into words, hadn't reminded her of the exact reason they were here.

A pair of mocking brows rose. 'So you weren't putting on an act? It wasn't part of the deal at all? Interesting!'

Simone snapped her teeth together and swung away. There was no way she could stop herself responding to him—and now he knew. He was going to glory in it—and she would be left looking a fool.

She headed for the *en suite* bathroom—a massive room, every inch of it tiled in an oyster colour. The D-shaped bath was sunken against one wall with the showerhead over it, and on the opposite wall were his-and-hers basins. As she stepped beneath the steaming jets, she closed her eyes and wished herself a million miles away.

Her body remained sensitised from Cade's intimate exploration, and the private heart of her still faintly throbbed. Damn Cade and his ability to do this. If only he hadn't uttered those cursed words she would have been happy, she would have felt like a new woman, would have looked forward to the next time.

But he had insisted on reminding her of the reason she was sharing his bed. She turned her face up to the shower, her eyes closed, and gave a squeal of alarm when she felt Cade's big hands around her waist. 'What are you doing?' she choked, dashing the water from her eyes, glaring at him with every ounce of anger she could dredge up.

'I need a shower too. I thought we'd save water.' But the smile on his lips told her that he was lying, that he simply wanted to sustain her torment.

'Well, I've finished, you're welcome to it,' she snapped.

'I don't think so,' he said before she could step out. 'You're mine, don't ever forget that. Mine in every sense of the word. And if I want you to share my shower then that's what you'll do.'

'I hate you!' she spat, her eyes enormous and vividly amethyst.

'If it was hate that turned you into an exciting temptress then I'm glad you hate me,' he returned with a smile. He squeezed shower gel into his palms and then handed her the bottle. 'How about we each wash the other off our skin? Although personally I would hate to get rid of the smell of you, you smell so gorgeous. We'll shower and then spend a lazy morning doing absolutely nothing. How does that sound?'

CHAPTER FIVE

CADE'S eyes were closed but it didn't mean he wasn't aware of Simone on the sun-lounger next to him. It was afternoon, and they'd had lunch on the deck and were now relaxing. They'd been swimming in the ocean that morning, and although Simone had at first been reluctant, apparently embarrassed by the way she had freely given herself to him earlier, she had eventually begun to enjoy herself.

Much to Cade's satisfaction. He wanted her to be happy and relaxed in his company, to appreciate all he intended doing for her, to hopefully fall in love with him again. He smiled at the thought of her ultimate downfall, and when he glanced at Simone she was watching him.

'Why are you smiling?' she enquired softly.

She lay on her back with her head turned towards him. A pair of very brief white shorts covered her hips, and a skinny top hid her enticing breasts. His heartrate increased simply by looking at her. Her limbs were long and golden, her skin soft and tempting to the touch. Already he wanted her again, but he knew he had to curb his urges or he would scare her away before his campaign had even started.

Even this morning had been a mistake. It hadn't been his intention to make love to her—not so soon and definitely not so completely. His hungry male hormones had run away with themselves; he'd been unable to stop them. Afterwards he had warned himself to be more careful in future.

He didn't tell Simone that he was picturing her retribution. Instead his smile widened. 'Who wouldn't smile when looking at such a vision of beauty?' he asked. 'I am totally amazed that your marriage didn't work out. Your husband must have been a fool to let you go.' And he meant it. She might have a devious mind, but to look at she was every man's dream—and in bed she was shameless.

Perhaps it was her Machiavellian nature that had frightened her husband away. Perhaps she had played her man along the same as she had him. The thought tightened his muscles, sent every sense whizzing into be-careful mode, reaffirming the fact that looks could be deceptive, that Simone Maxwell was not everything she appeared to be.

'Tell me about him,' he encouraged her when she remained silent, when her lips folded in on themselves and she turned her head away. Clearly the memories were painful.

Long seconds passed before she answered. 'His name was—is—Gerard. We met at a friend's birthday party. I didn't like him at first; I thought he was too loud. But he persisted in trying to get a date with me, and eventually I agreed.' She sat up, swinging her legs over the side of the sun-lounger, facing Cade.

Her knees almost brushed his arm, and he knew that all he had to do was lift his hand to touch her, to feel the smooth warmth of her skin, to experience a tingle through his fingertips. And then to want more. So he didn't touch her. He remained still and silent, his eyes on her face, waiting.

'To my surprise he was a pleasant and agreeable companion. He wasn't loud in my company; he was a considerate, nice guy. We began to see each other on a regular basis, and eventually he asked me to marry him.'

'Eventually? After how long?'

'A few months after you left.'

Too soon, he thought.

'Was he wealthy?'

Simone frowned. 'Why do you ask?'

Because he wanted to know whether she'd had plans for this poor guy's money as well! Nevertheless, he made himself smile. 'I just wondered, that's all. So what went wrong?' He pushed himself up on one elbow and continued to watch her face closely. Such an expressive face, such a beautiful face; it was no wonder he had once been madly in love with her.

She had fine, high cheekbones and beautiful wide eyes, thickly fringed. Sometimes she lowered those lashes to such an extent that they almost hid her fantastic eyes. Then she would look at him from beneath them, and he would feel his testosterone levels rise.

'He began spending far more time at work than he did with me,' she answered reluctantly. 'He always apologised, of course, he brought me gifts and flowers as compensation.'

'But I assume he was seeing another woman?' guessed Cade.

Simone frowned. 'How did you know?'

'Buying gifts is a standard guilt-move. How long did it go on for?'

But Simone didn't want to discuss the subject any more. She shook her head. 'Why all these questions?'

'You were my girl once, don't forget. I was your first boy-friend. I think I can claim some rights.'

'Rights?' she asked indignantly. 'When you ignored me the second you left Australia? When you wouldn't listen to anything I had to say? When you insisted on believing the worst of me? I don't have to tell you anything.' She sat that little bit straighter, bright indignation in her eyes, giving an excellent performance at being the injured party.

She was in the wrong profession, thought Cade—she ought to be an actress. But as now wasn't the time to bring up the past he let it go, saying instead, 'True, and I shouldn't be asking these questions. What do you think—should we take the boat out instead?'

It sat there invitingly—a top-of-the-range single-hulled sailing boat, thirty-six feet long—and already he had organised provisions to be stowed on board just in case.

But there was doubt in Simone's eyes.

'You're afraid of me at such close quarters?' he guessed. 'There's no need. I promise I won't do anything that you're not comfortable with.'

Simone knew that behind Cade's smile was intent. She couldn't trust him. Or was it herself she didn't trust? She had been truly stunned by the depth of her feelings earlier. She had never imagined, not in her wildest dreams, that she would ever share Cade's bed again.

But actually she would love to go out on the boat. It had been so long since she'd done such a thing, even though sailing boats were her business. And surely Cade was a man of honour, despite what had already happened between them? He knew how she felt about him kissing her. She closed her eyes suddenly. That was the trouble—he knew *exactly* how she felt!

But she could be strong. She knew now what she was up against. She had to be strong for her own peace of mind.

She nodded. 'I guess it would be OK. At least it'll be cooler out there.'

Half an hour later Simone asked herself why she had ever

thought that she would be strong enough to resist temptation. Cade was temptation personified! He had the power to draw her in, slow inch by slow inch, until she was begging him to make love to her.

Deep down inside she hungered for him to kiss her, to share that big, round bed in the master cabin. She had taken a tour of the boat as he'd gently eased it from its mooring, and her heart had beat a rapid tattoo against her breastbone at the thought of Cade making love to her there.

It was definitely a bed made for sharing. The satin sheets were to-die-for, and she could just imagine…

Simone let her thoughts go no further. This was insanity.

On deck she sat as far away from Cade as she could. He was using the engine rather than the sails, so there was no need for her to help. Nevertheless she was still vitally aware of him, so aware that she was in danger of giving herself away.

When he dropped anchor she felt a quiver of unease. There was no escape from his *very big* presence. It was odd that, with all the wide-open space around them, she felt so enclosed. The fact was that there was simply nowhere to run. A few metres of deck and that was all.

'Are you all right, Simone? You look a little pale.'

Heavens, he must never guess at the feelings panicking through her. He'd need no more than a hint to take advantage. She smiled. 'I'm fine. Would you like a drink—tea? Coffee? I'll make it.' Anything to put space between them.

'Actually I was thinking of something a little stronger. Wine, perhaps. There's some already chilling. But you don't have to do it, I'll—'

'No, I want to,' insisted Simone, and she fled to the galley. When she opened the fridge, and saw that it was well stocked with both food and drink, Simone knew that Cade had planned an evening of seduction and she cursed herself for walking into his trap.

She quickly found two glasses, and in the shaded part of the deck Cade did the honours. 'What shall we drink to?' he asked, with an odd, unnerving smile. 'Good health? To our new partnership, perhaps? Or simply to us—to old friendships?' He tilted his glass towards her. 'Old friendships it is. May they flourish and survive.'

Simone lifted her glass, but she couldn't see how any sort of relationship could prosper. He was helping her out of a sticky situation, yes, but the payment he'd demanded was exorbitant. Cade had said he wouldn't touch her unless it was what she wanted, but—and she hated to use the word—he had bought her. In her own mind she knew that he would keep his word, but the idea that he could use her whenever the mood took him both unnerved and excited her.

He was dressed all in white, the same as she was, expensive shorts exposing powerfully muscled legs. A designer T-shirt emphasised more well-honed muscles, broad shoulders, a long body and narrow hips. All features she was uncomfortably familiar with.

They sat in silence for a few minutes, Simone acutely aware of Cade looking at her.

She wished he would speak—say something—anything, instead of this steady appraisal. It not only sent trickles of alarm through her system, but hunger as well. He was not a man who could be dismissed easily. He could be the only person in a room and fill it with his presence. She had experienced it first hand on many occasions. Now it was a hundred times worse.

'A penny for them.'

She turned startled eyes to his face. He probably knew

exactly what she was thinking. But she answered neverthe-less. 'As a matter of fact, I was wondering why I'm here. I'm sure pleasure trips weren't part of the deal.'

Cade seemed to find difficulty in stopping his lips from smiling. 'So what exactly did you expect from our relation-ship? Apart from the money, of course.'

When she didn't answer, when she stared at him belliger-ently, he went on, 'What precisely did you think a mistress did?—spent time in her man's bed and that was all? Maybe that's the dictionary definition, and I can accommodate you in that direction—right now, if it's what you wish. But my interpretation—in our case, at least—is of a woman who shares all of her man's pleasures. Not only physical, but other parts of his life as well.'.

'In other words,' said Simone, 'I'd be your wife in all but name.'

'Something of the sort,' he admitted with an insouciant shrug. 'Except that at the end of the term we both walk free.'

Free. *Free?* Surely he knew that would be an impos-sibility? She would be scarred for life. She would never be rid of him. He would live in her mind for ever, even if she never saw him again.

She had no doubt that sharing his bed earlier was only the tip of the iceberg. He would want—no, he would demand—so much from her that she would be a pitiless wreck by the end of it all.

When he eventually tired of their arrangement, she'd have a business to run but no spirit left in her to do it. Did he know that? Was it his ultimate aim—to let her think he was helping, but in reality to break her and then take over the business for himself? His more than generous offer was nothing but a form of punishment for the way her father had double-crossed him.

Her mind spun dizzyingly, and she felt her hand tremble as she took another sip of the excellent Pinot Noir.

'You look disturbed,' he said. 'You're not having misgivings? A deal is a deal in my eyes. Unless, of course, you want to say to hell with everything and find some other way of financing your future?' Golden eyes locked into hers, challenging her, disturbing her, making her stiffen her resolve.

'I'm not disturbed, Cade, you're imagining things,' Simone stated, trying to keep calm, but feeling tension in the air thick enough to slice with a knife.

Simone was disturbed by Cade and their situation, but she sure as hell wasn't going to let him know it. 'It would be a pleasure to share your bed, Cade,' she declared, her chin high, her steady eyes daring him to say anything else.

To his credit he didn't, but his lips twitched, and Simone knew that he felt he had scored.

For the rest of the trip—circling one of the many incredibly beautiful islands that made up the Whitsundays, eating a light meal of cold chicken and salad, finishing the bottle of wine—he kept their conversation on an impersonal basis. They talked instead about what he was hoping to achieve—apparently no less than the finest yacht-charter business in the area.

Simone was duly impressed. His big ideas were going to cost a small fortune, and she was overwhelmed that he was clearly putting so much effort into the business. It didn't make sense, but she couldn't afford to question it, not if she wanted to keep afloat. She knew that selling her body was a huge price to pay, but the man in question was Cade Dupont. There was no other man on the planet who could ask her such a thing and no other man for whom she would relent.

The whole of the time they'd been out on the water she had expected him to whisk her down to the cabin and demand part-payment. In fact, she'd wanted him to make love to her. Being so close to him, inhaling the sheer maleness of him, feeling sensuality dripping from each of his pores, had created a hunger far deeper than she had ever imagined she would feel for this man again. And when he hadn't so much as kissed her she had felt stupidly disappointed. So much so that she had felt like taking the initiative herself.

Which would have been even more stupid.

But now the day had ended. They'd enjoyed an evening meal on the deck outside the house, they'd watched the perpetual movement of the ocean, listened to a few bird calls, and eventually Cade had suggested they retire for the night.

It felt strange, sharing the same room, showering and then brushing her teeth while Cade did the same at her side. The only difference was that she donned a robe after her shower. Cade stood proudly naked. She tried not to look at him, but it was impossible. Was there ever such a perfect specimen of virility?

So many serious sensations waltzed through her body that they made her breathless, and she wanted to leap on him, beg him to make love to her there and then. She knew that they would make love once they went to bed, it was inevitable— but she didn't want to wait, she wanted him now!

His eyes met hers through the mirrored wall behind the hand basins. He knew. He knew exactly what she was thinking. Simone flicked her eyes to her own reflection and saw hot hunger, saw purple eyes that were glazed with passion, and a face glowing with primitive need.

'Shall we?' he asked quietly, holding his hand out.

'Shall we what?' She was embarrassed that he had read her body signals so clearly.

'Retire to bed, of course. You've had a long day, you must be tired.'

Simone knew that he was humouring her, knew that the second they were in bed their bodies would come together and all hell would break loose. She turned away so that he could no longer see her face. 'Yes, I am tired,' she agreed, but even to her own ears her voice sounded pathetically weak.

Ignoring his still-outstretched hand, she walked through to the massive bedroom with its cream-carpeted floor and a bed big enough to sleep three. She could feel her cheeks flaming at the very thought of what was going to happen there. She stood at the end, unable to go any further, and felt Cade's hands gently lift the robe from her shoulders.

He was an amazing man. He could be both gentle and fiercely demanding in the same second. Her heart threatened to leap out of her chest, the pulse in her throat threatened to choke her, and yet all she could do was stand there and suffer his touch.

She kept her eyes closed, even though there was no mirror in front her. Somehow it felt easier to let her emotions run free if she couldn't see her surroundings, couldn't see the man who was at this very moment sliding his hands around her, cupping her breasts, teasing her nipples as only he knew how to. Against her she felt his fierce need, and without even thinking she twisted herself around in his arms and offered her mouth to his.

His tasted of passion, of primitive hunger as deep as her own, and with a guttural groan he lifted her into his arms and laid her none too gently on the bed. What happened after that was a feverish mixture of need and thirst as his hands tormented and her body responded.

Cade didn't know how he had managed to keep his hands off Simone for so many hours. Making love to her this morning had woken a whole galaxy of primitive emotions. And he wanted more. Much more.

He loved the satin feel of her skin, the delicious clean smell of her: sexy woman and shy girl mixed into one. He loved it when she squirmed beneath his touch, when all he had to do was stroke one hard, sensitive nipple to make her writhe on the bed.

'Make love to me, Cade,' she breathed. 'Make love to me.'

Her eyes were closed, she was in a world where nothing mattered except release from the serious sensations chasing their way through her beautiful body. He had never seen her quite so hungry for him. And, Lord help him, he'd never wanted her more either. She was his for the taking. What should have been a power struggle was proving tremendously easy.

He wanted to take his time, make her suffer some more, but he couldn't. Her excitement was his excitement. Her need was his. His whole body set on fire with an incredible build-up of desperate feelings. He couldn't wait. He had to take her. Now!

He exulted in the fact that he was able to reduce her to this, to make her dependent on him for her pleasure, to make her ache and hunger for him every minute of the day—as he had once ached for her, and still did. She was an extraordinary woman and, as the passion built between them, soon Cade could take no more. He collapsed on top of Simone, and despite his own convulsions he could feel her still shuddering beneath him.

In the middle of the night he woke and took her again. And again. Not once did Simone object. She even initiated some of their love play. When she sucked and nibbled his nipples, when she trailed kisses down the hard length of his chest and stomach, creeping inexorably towards her goal, he experienced a high of excitement that he had rarely felt before.

He'd had a couple of girlfriends in England, yes, but none

had been as sensationally successful in arousing his libido as Simone was at this moment.

Cade was inclined to be impatient; he wanted results straight away. Simone's complete capitulation should have been an answer to his dreams—ironically, he didn't feel that way. She was too willing, too compliant, too soon. Building her up to knock her down had been part of the plan. He had never in his wildest dreams expected her to surrender so soon and so divinely.

On the other hand wouldn't her instant response work to his advantage? Wouldn't her downfall be even more spectacular? Somewhere at the back of his mind lurked vague unease. Things weren't going exactly the way he'd wanted. He was getting a great deal of pleasure, yes, but he had expected to take his time—not this rapid explosion of feelings that sent them both into orbit.

When Simone woke she wondered at first whether she had dreamt all that had happened last night. But then the tenderness in parts of her body told her that it had been exciting reality. She only had to think about what had happened to feel a resurrection of stunningly beautiful feelings.

She had the bed to herself. She must have been sound asleep when Cade got up, because she hadn't heard him or felt him move. Being worn out was the obvious reason! Acute embarrassment took the place of pleasure. How could she have given herself to him so freely? Why hadn't she found the strength to hide the way her body reacted to his?

Disgusted with herself, she trailed through to the bathroom and tried to shower the smell of Cade from her skin. She scrubbed and scrubbed until she was satisfied, and then dressed in a pair of long cotton trousers and a T-shirt. No exposed flesh today, nothing to tempt him.

She found Cade in a superbly appointed study area, his feet up on the desk, a telephone to his ear. 'Yes, that's right— ASAP or I go elsewhere.' He switched off the phone and looked at her. 'So you made it. I began to think you were going to sleep all day.'

'What time is it?' asked Simone with a frown. She hadn't looked at her watch; she hadn't even put it on.

'Just turned eleven,' came the careless drawl.

'Good heavens! Why didn't you wake me?'

'Because you looked so beautiful in your sleep. You've not changed, Simmy. You still lie stretched out like a trusting baby.'

His use of his pet name for her made Simone bring her head up sharp. 'You stood watching me?'

He inclined his head. 'I was sorely tempted to wake you and make some more of that fantastic love. But then I decided to save that pleasure for later.'

His voice had dropped a couple of octaves, coming from somewhere deep in his throat, making her toes curl and her pulses flutter. It was safer not to respond, not to let him know that her senses were still fine-tuned.

'That was the boat builders,' Cade said, indicating the call he had just ended.

Simone frowned. 'You've placed a definite order?'

Cade inclined his head.

'Without confirming it with me?'

'My money, my decision,' he declared. 'Do you have a problem with that, Simone?'

Simone realised that she was in no position to argue. But she wasn't going to stand there and take everything he threw at her. 'Didn't our conversation yesterday mean anything? Surely you're aware how I feel?'

'Oh yes, I'm aware all right,' he answered. 'What would

you like me to do—consult you every step of the way? Waste valuable time? Surely you realise that time means money? I've ordered the best motor-yachts that money can buy, from the most prestigious company in Australia. Do you object to that?'

His eyes were a force to be reckoned with. Gone was the drowsy arousal of last night, and in its place was sharp efficiency.

Simone lifted her shoulders in reluctant acceptance. But she couldn't help wondering exactly how much more he would demand of her in payment for an outlay that had obviously run into millions of dollars. She couldn't see him walking away at the end of the day leaving her to get on with it. He wouldn't be a silent partner.

He would demand more of her, and the trouble was she didn't know what to expect.

CHAPTER SIX

'SIMONE! At last. Have you any idea how long I've been trying to reach you?'

'Hi, Ros,' said Simone, closing her eyes, knowing her friend would want a blow-by-blow account of all that had been happening in her life, but not wanting to tell her.

'Why've you had your phone turned off?'

'The battery was flat,' she explained. That at least was true.

'So where are you?' demanded Ros. 'There's a message on your office answering-machine—in a strange man's voice, I might add—saying that the company's closed for upgrade. What's that supposed to mean? Where did you get money to do a thing like that? I rang your home number as well and your father said that you'd gone off with a man. He didn't sound too pleased. So, come on, give. I want every intriguing detail.'

'Do you have a few hours?' groaned Simone.

'As long as you like,' answered Ros. 'Where are you? I'll come over.'

'No!' answered Simone in panic. The last thing she wanted was Ros sticking her very enquiring nose into her relationship with Cade.

'Simone! What's wrong?'

'Nothing,' she answered. 'Except that Cade Dupont's back

in Australia.' There was no point in hiding it from Ros, as sure as the sky was blue she would find out one way or another.

'Cade!' shrieked Ros. 'Are you two together again?'

'Definitely not!' Simone claimed fiercely.

'So where are you? Are you living with him? There's clearly more to this than you're telling me, Simone.'

'No, there isn't,' insisted Simone.

'So why are you with him?'

'It's business; he's investing. There's a lot to sort out.' Hell, if her friend ever found out the truth she'd have a field day.

'I bet there is!' exclaimed Ros. 'You and Cade were hot stuff; I can't see him investing and not getting anything out of it. Does he want a relationship with you again? Jeez, this is exciting. Let's have coffee together somewhere, and—'

'Look Ros, I'm sorry, but I have to go now. I'll ring you when this thing's over.' And she ended the call.

'Who was that?'

Cade had walked into the room behind her, and Simone couldn't help wondering how much of the conversation he'd heard. It was unusual for her to cut her friend short. They normally chatted for hours. But she didn't want to tell Ros about her arrangement with Cade, because she knew what her reaction would be. The situation was far too humiliating to confess to her friend.

'Ros Fletcher,' she answered finally.

His eyes narrowed and she could see his brain working. 'Your old friend Ros? Do you still see her?'

Simone nodded.

'So why don't you invite her over?'

Intense violet eyes flashed. 'Do you really think I want her to know what's going on between us?'

'A mistress used to be a very honourable profession in days of yore,' he announced, his lips twitching in amusement.

'Maybe,' she snapped. 'But I hardly think Ros would see it that way.'

'Perhaps not,' he agreed. 'But she would certainly approve of us getting back together, don't you think? She needn't know about our little—er—plan.'

'Get lost!' cried Simone angrily. 'Ros isn't stupid, she'd soon see that you're using me for your own mercenary pleasure.'

To her dismay Cade smiled. 'Maybe you're right. We don't want people intruding on our congenial activities, do we? You look as though you could do with a good strong drink,' he said, a humorous twist to his lips. 'Or maybe a kiss will make you feel better.' Without giving her time to object, he enclosed her in his arms.

Simone's struggles were in vain. She flung her head back and glared, but all he did was smile. Seconds later his mouth laid claim to hers. She wanted to snub him; she wanted to make him see that he couldn't take her whenever he felt like it. But her inner body made nonsense of her thoughts. Hot blood raced madly through her system, her lips springing to life beneath his.

But as soon as the kiss began it was disappointingly over. 'Better now?' asked Cade, as one would after kissing a child's wound. 'I thought we'd go shopping.'

'For what?' asked Simone, disappointment making her tone sharp. As far as she could see, there was nothing they needed. Except perhaps a journey forward in time to where her business was running successfully again and Cade was out of her life.

If that ever happened! He might not consider her being a temporary mistress was enough. He might decide to stay in

Australia long-term. He might want more than a fair share of her business.

Simone didn't realise how much her thoughts were reflected in her eyes until Cade said, 'You may as well get used to the idea that you're stuck with me for some considerable time. It's no use getting wound up about it. Come on, let's go.'

Cade's idea of shopping was very different from Simone's. She had thought they would go into town, and was shocked when he drove to a small, private airfield where a helicopter sat waiting. Her eyes widened. 'What's this? What have you got planned now?' She was deeply suspicious of his motives. Cade didn't do anything that couldn't be exploited to his own advantage.

'I thought a trip into Brisbane might prove a welcome diversion. Isn't retail therapy what most women like?'

'Maybe, but not this one,' Simone assured him. 'I don't need anything.'

'You mean you'd rather stay at home with me?' His lips twitched as he spoke, and Simone could have slapped him.

'I'd rather not be anywhere with you,' she answered instead.

'You certainly didn't feel that way last night. But since you're stuck with me you may as well make the most of it. Hop in, enjoy the ride.'

Simone might have enjoyed it, had she been with someone different. It seemed to her that Cade Dupont was hell-bent on making her enjoy herself, whether she felt like it or not. Simone had never flown before. There'd been no need. When you lived somewhere as beautiful as she did, why take a holiday in another country? When she went to Brisbane, or even Sydney, she always drove, perhaps staying overnight in a motel on the way.

Now, though, she discovered a fear that made her curl

against Cade and bury her face in his chest. She felt foolish, but was unable to help herself.

'Whatever's wrong?' he asked, and a firm finger under her chin turned her face up to his.

'I'm scared,' she managed to gasp.

Strong arms enclosed her. 'It's perfectly safe, and really quite amazing, when you get used to it. Look how translucent the ocean is from up here—look how green the islands are. Millions of people would give their eye-teeth to be in your shoes, to experience first-hand a bird's-eye view of the Whitsundays. You've swum in the waters, you've dived and snorkelled, and now you're seeing them from a completely different angle. You're a lucky woman, Simone.'

She could almost believe it. Except that luck hadn't played a very big part in her life. For the moment, though, she preferred to forget that. She wanted to take pleasure in being held so close to Cade's chest that she could feel the drum of his heartbeat. It was powerful and strong, like the man he was. He made her feel better; he surprisingly made her forget her initial fear, and she began to enjoy.

Damn! She didn't want to enjoy. She was being forced into Cade's life by the sheer foolishness of her father's habits. She was being compelled to protect her mother's beloved company by selling her body to a man who had no compunction about using her.

He could be nice, yes, like he was at this moment, but inside his handsome skin was a man with no heart. He would let her believe he was helping her out, but at the end of the day she would be the loser.

This thought alone had her pulling away from him. 'I'm all right now.'

'If you're sure?'

His smiling glance told her that he was well aware of the thoughts swirling in her head. He knew that she hated him seeing her weakness. If she wasn't careful, he would have such a hold over her that her life would never be her own again.

They landed on the helipad of one of Brisbane's top hotels. Typical Cade, thought Simone. It had clearly been pre-arranged, because there were drinks waiting for them. They had views over the river and Story Bridge, and afterwards they strolled through the shopping area.

Cade insisted on ushering her into an exclusive dress-shop, and sat there either approving or disapproving as she tried on what seemed like hundreds of outfits.

Actually it was rather fun, she decided, twirling this way and that in front of him. 'How about this one?' she asked as she emerged in a short, flirty dress held up by sheer willpower.

Cade pursed his lips and shook his head. 'Too dangerous.' But his eyes twinkled all the same.

'Or this?' A beautiful ball-gown. She had never possessed such a beautiful gown in all her life; she had never needed one. This was made of something soft and seductive, in a pale-vanilla colour with spaghetti straps and a tiny waist. She felt more elegant than she'd ever felt before and it pleased her to see Cade's reaction.

His eyes narrowed, and he actually looked stunned by the transformation. 'We'll take that one,' he said softly.

'But I'll never wear it,' she protested. It was a lot of fun trying on all these clothes, but she couldn't possibly let him buy any of them when they would sit in her wardrobe unused.

'Don't worry, I'll take you somewhere where you will,' he insisted, nodding his head to the assistant, who hadn't been able to take her eyes off Cade ever since he'd stepped into the shop.

He did look fantastic, thought Simone, in his sharply

pressed trousers and a crisp light-grey shirt. He was over six-feet tall and handsome to boot, but it was his thickly fringed golden eyes that appealed to most people. One look from them and you felt special, as though you were the only person in the room.

Cade felt an inexplicable pleasure in seeing Simone model the various outfits. She had no idea how beautiful she was, how extraordinarily sexy. Her cheeks were delicately coloured, giving away her embarrassment, even though she made no show of it.

He found himself hungering to take her to bed. Her bright eyes and some of the poses she'd struck swept his male hormones into a mini whirlwind. Getting her to try on so many clothes was giving him the chance to look at Simone without her questioning his motives—but it also created havoc inside him.

Suddenly he wanted the day to end. He wanted her to himself. He wanted her to model for him in the exclusive privacy of the beach house. He wanted to dress her himself, to touch, to stroke, to feel, to… He dared not let his thoughts go any further, not here in this hushed, elegant place.

By the time they'd finished Simone had a complete new wardrobe set to one side, but when he arranged to have them delivered to the hotel she held up her hands in protest. 'I don't need all these new clothes, Cade. It's been fun, but—'

He refused to listen. Perhaps she didn't need them—not in her eyes, anyway. But it had been such a pleasure to watch her—she probably hadn't spent anything on herself for ages—that he couldn't possibly disappoint her.

Anyway, he had plans. Simone was going to be wined and dined in the most elegant of places. He was going to show her what sort of life she could have led if she hadn't tricked him.

In that way her downfall, when it came, would be very spectacular indeed. Already he could see that she was warming towards him, and she was most certainly appreciating the luxuries he was introducing into her life.

Later they went for a dinner cruise on a paddle steamer, where he insisted she wear one of her new dresses, and when they eventually made their way back to the hotel and the helicopter it was dark.

Brisbane at night was stunning from above: points of light everywhere, some moving, some still. They were able to pick out the river, the bridge and the cruise boats, and Simone clung to him as they looked down.

He wasn't sure whether it was because she was still scared of flying, or whether the pleasure of the day made her relax in his company. Whatever, it was all to the good.

Cade stroked a strand of hair back from Simone's face, letting his fingers linger on her cheek. She didn't stop him; in fact her hand came over his and held it there, much to his satisfaction. Making her his mistress had been one thing, but getting her to actually need him, want him, was another. He sought complete capitulation. He wanted her to be unable to live without him.

The fact that she would gain a successful company out of it didn't bother him; it was her mind he wanted to play with. He wanted to crush her the way he had been crushed. An eye for an eye, and all that.

It didn't occur to Cade that he was beginning to feel something for Simone—that even now, touching her like this, was not a deliberate attempt to seduce her but a very real need for physical contact. As far as he was concerned, the only feelings he had were of lust for her beautiful body.

Simone felt surprisingly content. The day had been a dream

in more ways than one. Cade had treated her as though she were someone special, someone who meant something to him. She hadn't enjoyed herself so much in a long time.

The beautiful clothes—which she didn't need and didn't want—had been totally unexpected. She had felt like a million dollars, parading for his benefit, but she couldn't actually see that she would have any opportunities to wear them. Her social life was too casual.

Her thoughts pulled up short. Except that she would be spending the next however-how-long with Cade—and his lifestyle was totally different from hers. He was a high flier who dressed accordingly. This had to be why she had been treated to a whole new wardrobe.

'Were you ashamed of me in the clothes I wore?' she asked sharply, even as the thought occurred to her.

Cade's frown was instant. 'What are you talking about?'

'All the new outfits! There has to be a reason why you spent so much money on me.'

'You always look gorgeous, Simone, no matter what you wear,' he said softly. 'I thought you deserved to be treated. It's as simple as that. I had no ulterior motive.'

Unsure whether to believe him, Simone turned her attention back to the view from the window. The lights of the city were disappearing as they followed the coastline. Other than the lingering aftermath of the sunset, there was not much to see.

It was her heart that bothered her. It was thundering like a giant beast in her breast. All because Cade had said she was gorgeous. It had probably been nothing more than a figure of speech. On the other hand it could mean that he was warming towards her.

And pigs might fly!

She would never be able to convince him that she'd had

nothing to do with her father's plan all those years ago. What chance had she unless her father himself admitted the truth? And that was about as likely as her jumping from this helicopter and not getting killed.

'Are you worried about something?' Cade asked quietly.

'Of course not,' answered Simone quickly. She didn't want to spoil this day by bringing up the thorny subject that had sent him away in the first place.

'You were deep in thought all of a sudden. Was I the subject?'

She couldn't answer; she couldn't possibly tell him that he was never out of them.

'Perhaps you were wondering whether I was going to do this?' Tilting her face up to meet his, he took her lips in a kiss that sent her spinning, as though the helicopter itself had moved off its axis and was throwing them around in a void.

What the pilot must be thinking she didn't know, and for the moment didn't care. She was growing used to Cade's kisses— no, that was wrong. How could she ever get used to them? They were a law unto themselves, always different, always challenging, always creating new and incredible sensations.

When their tongues touched, when she tasted him, when she explored his mouth, all hell broke loose inside her, and she wanted the journey to end so that they could go to bed and make amazing love.

It was strange, she thought, how quickly she had accepted the situation. From being totally appalled at the idea of becoming Cade's mistress, she was already settling into the part.

Suddenly hating the thought of what she was doing, Simone struggled to free herself. 'I don't want this, Cade. Not here, not now, not in front of the pilot.'

'Eddie won't mind,' he said, and he pulled her head close to his again. 'Don't forget,' he whispered, his voice going even lower, 'He doesn't know the real reason you're partnering me. He thinks we're true lovers.'

To add credence to his words, he captured her mouth again, his hands moving to touch her already-burgeoning breasts, to torment one tingling nipple after the other, and to promise her she wouldn't get a second's sleep that night.

Which she didn't.

Except that it didn't happen quite how she expected. Simone had thought that once they were back at the beach house they would rip each other's clothes off and fall into bed, both so hungry for each other's bodies that they couldn't help themselves.

What she hadn't counted on was Cade's incredible self-control.

'Perhaps a drink before we—er—retire?' he suggested with a half smile, indicating that she sit down.

Simone crushed her searing emotions and sank into a leather chair, kicking off her shoes and curling her toes in the deep-pile rug that graced the wooden floor. She watched Cade as he opened a bottle of wine and filled two crystal glasses. He had always been the man of her dreams, always would be, whether anything further materialised or not.

She ought to have known better than to marry Gerard. It had been on the rebound from Cade—a man she'd never expected to see again. A man who at this moment was sending her heartrate soaring and pulses dancing all over the place.

Gerard had never managed to make her feel quite like this. And when she'd discovered that he had been having an affair, that he'd thought so little of their marriage that he was tempted to seek pleasure elsewhere, it had made her wonder whether any man was to be trusted.

In fact after that she had made a conscious decision never

to marry again. Not until she found true love with a man who respected her. She had truly loved Cade, and had thought he loved her—until he had refused to believe in her innocence and left her, proving that his love had not been as strong as her own. Maybe he'd never really loved her. Would she ever know?

But, whether it was love or not that she was feeling now, she didn't want them to sit here like two civilised people. She wanted Cade's body moulded to hers, she wanted to feel him inside her, she wanted relief from her tormented emotions.

'What's wrong?'

Cade's voice invaded her thoughts, and Simone looked at him with shocked wide eyes. Was she so transparent that he could see what was in her mind? 'Nothing,' she murmured.

'What were you thinking?' He walked towards her and settled in the companion armchair, standing their glasses on a sand-coloured, leather-topped table in front of them.

'Nothing,' she said again.

'Were you wondering what you are doing here with me? Is it getting too much for you? Would you like to forget our arrangement and go back to the way you were?'

'No!' said Simone quickly.

'Then perhaps it's me you want.' A note of amusement entered his voice. 'You expected more when we arrived home?'

Simone felt swift colour scorch her cheeks. 'I know better than that,' she declared aggressively. 'I know that I'm here for your pleasure, nothing more.'

'Good, I'm glad you realise it.' Cade's eyes hardened on hers as he settled into his chair. He took a sip of wine. 'Excellent stuff, this,' he commented. 'Try yours.'

Simone already felt heady with desire, if she drank her wine as well it could prove disastrous. Nevertheless she took a tiny sip and then replaced the glass back on the table. She couldn't understand what was happening. They had gone from being almost lovers on the helicopter to strangers now. Cade was certainly playing a game with her.

'Tell me your thoughts, Simone,' he said after a moment or two's silence.

'You know what they are,' she protested, avoiding looking at him directly, but able to see their reflections in the floor-to-ceiling windows opposite. He was watching her closely, and she felt fresh colour redden her face.

'No, I don't, tell me.'

'I hate myself for wanting you,' she admitted in a husky voice that sounded nothing like her own. 'I went along with your game because I had no choice, but I never believed that I'd—*enjoy* being your lover.'

'Shall I let you into a little secret?' he asked, seeming to find it difficult to stop his lips from smiling. 'I enjoy you being my lover as well.'

Which was a totally different thing from enjoying *loving* her, thought Simone. He enjoyed the physical side of it, he enjoyed seeing how far he could take her. But he was still a man doing her a favour. He would take and take from her until she had nothing left to give.

That was a certainty.

CHAPTER SEVEN

SIMONE was thinking about leaving the pool when Cade joined her. The first she knew of his presence was the splash he made when he dived into the water. Not exactly a splash but a perfectly executed entry. Like everything he did in life, Cade was a first-class swimmer. She knew that he'd been encouraged to train for the Olympics, but had decided against it as it would have taken up too much of his time and he'd wanted other things out of life.

'Business done,' he said as he surfaced beside her with a smile that created havoc with her senses. 'I'm yours for the rest of the day.'

Simone smiled weakly. Hers! What did that mean? Last night, when she had hungered for him in bed beside her, he had shut himself away to make phone calls to England. He'd not given her so much as a kiss before she'd retired, leaving her in a state of unfulfilled limbo until she'd finally fallen asleep.

And when she'd woken this morning he'd been sleeping the sleep of the innocent. She had stood by the bed for a moment, watching him. He'd looked vulnerable, his arms thrown back like a baby, the sheets down to his waist. His hard, tanned chest with its scattering of dark hairs had tempted her to touch, to nuzzle her face into it, to kiss, to arouse, to...

She had turned away in disgust. Anyone would think their arrangement was about nothing but self-indulgence. When he had got up he'd shut himself away in his office again and Simone had decided to make use of the pool.

Cade trod water, his gorgeous, golden eyes smiling into hers, sending wave after wave of instant desire racing through her veins. Heavens, she was becoming foolishly attracted. Wearing her heart on her sleeve would give him an advantage. She had to pretend, like she had never pretended before, that he meant nothing to her.

'So what do you suggest we do?' she asked. 'It doesn't seem right that we spend all our time seeking pleasure when there's a business to be built up. I think we ought to order new brochures. Get them sent out as soon as possible. Upgrade the website. There's a lot to organise.'

'All of which I've already considered,' he told her.

'But have you done anything about it?' She hoped he hadn't; she desperately needed some input into her newly transformed business. She wouldn't be half the woman she thought she was if she let him take over completely.

His eyes rested on hers for several long moments. 'Not yet. I—'

'Then let me,' she cut in urgently. 'I'm not used to sitting around doing nothing.'

'You look remarkably pretty doing nothing.' One hand came up to touch her cheek, to stroke a strand of damp hair behind her ear. Then he hooked his hand behind her head and pressed a cold, damp kiss to her lips before smiling some more. 'Making love is so much more exciting, don't you think?'

'Is that all I'm good for?' Her violet eyes grew hot with resentment, and she backed away.

'Didn't you miss me in bed last night?' he asked softly.

'Like a thorn in my side,' she snapped, unwilling to admit exactly how much she had missed him. The bed had felt empty. It was so huge that she'd tossed and turned a long time before she'd finally settled.

'The time difference makes it difficult to keep contact with the other side of the world,' he acknowledged with a wry twist to his lips. 'Something has to give.'

Simone tossed her head. 'Don't worry yourself on my account.'

'I can't believe you didn't miss me,' he murmured. 'Maybe I'm not doing enough to…' Even as he spoke a lazy finger trailed down the length of her throat and over the gently rounded curves of her breasts that rose above her swimsuit.

'Don't even say it,' warned Simone, backing away as fresh rivers of sensation rose and devoured. Letting Cade fuel her like this was sheer madness—yet she was powerless to stop him. One touch and she was putty in his hands. One touch and burning desire traced its way through every bone in her body.

'You mean actions speak louder than words?' he suggested, sliding his hand lower until her breast was fully cupped and he was in a position to expertly tease her nipple with thumb and forefinger.

Despite trying her hardest to pretend she felt nothing, Simone grew crazy with desire, the heat between her legs reaching an unbearable pitch. Perhaps Cade had conjured up a devious plan, knowing that yesterday evening, after the fantastic day they'd spent in Brisbane, he could have taken her any time he wanted.

He was so right. She had been ready for him, desperately disappointed when he'd left her strictly alone, and now her whole body ached to be possessed. Unable to stop herself, she lifted her face to his, giving a tiny gasp when she saw her own desperate desire mirrored there.

His eyes were the darkest gold she had ever seen. He looked almost in pain as they met hers, and by mutual consent their mouths came together in a kiss that sent vibrations through her body such as she had never felt before.

It lasted for no more than a few seconds, but in that short space of time Simone had foolishly let Cade see that she was his for the taking.

When he dragged his mouth away, when he set her a few inches apart, when his hunger had gone to be replaced by a serious expression, Simone began to wonder whether she hadn't imagined what she had seen.

He was clearly playing with her emotions, seeing how far he could go before she crumbled and gave him her everything. He wanted her to genuinely fall for him all over again. The fact that it was costing him a small fortune to do so didn't enter Simone's head. All she could think of was the fact that Cade wanted to hurt her like he never had before.

Nevertheless when he folded her in his strong arms all such thoughts fled. His kiss was so fierce and so demanding that it spiralled her into ecstasy, and everything else was forgotten.

Gasping, her chest heaving, Simone opened her mouth to drag in much-needed air, only to have it plundered by Cade's tongue, to feel an explosion of unreal sensations that rocked her off her feet. With one fluid movement he swept her up against his magnificent chest and carried her towards the steps at the end of the pool.

Here he set her down on one of the sturdy sunbeds. Simone could see his chest heaving in conjunction with her own, and it was only a matter of seconds before he peeled off her swimsuit and stepped out of his own shorts. With his eyes never deviating from hers, he lowered himself over her.

At the same moment the telephone rang, the outdoor bell

sounding strident and persistent, shattering the moment. There was no ignoring it. Cade uttered a curse beneath his breath and pushed himself to his feet. 'I'll be right back,' he warned. 'Don't move.'

But the moment had passed. Simone knew she could no more lie naked and wait than she could fly to the moon. She got up and fled to the outdoor shower and changing area, and by the time Cade returned she had sluiced down her body, roughly dried herself and, wrapped in a turquoise caftan, was making her way back to the house.

'What's this?' he growled.

'I've changed my mind,' said Simone, her voice no more than a husky whisper, and carried on walking.

But she didn't get away with it. Cade followed, and just as she reached the bedroom he caught her from behind and whipped the robe off with one deft movement.

'Remember, Simone, you don't get to choose when or where,' he grated. 'On the other hand—' a shadow crossed his face '—I have no wish to take a woman who's not willing. Don't think the party's over, though, because I can assure you it isn't.'

For the rest of the morning Simone avoided Cade. In fact, she didn't see him all day. When she got fed up with her own company and went in search of him, he had disappeared. His car had gone too.

Simone knew that she ought to feel glad she was being given a reprieve, but, oddly, she missed him. She'd had enough time on her own; she wanted Cade now. Or at the very least she wanted company.

She made her way to his office and browsed through some of the papers he had left on the desk. Notes were scribbled in his hand—firm, bold writing in black ink, suggesting a man very much in control of himself and everything he did. Even if she hadn't known it was Cade's handwriting, she would have said that the words were written by a man with a very positive attitude towards life.

There were times and dates that meant nothing to her—clearly relating to his activities on the other side of the world. But in a separate pile were notes about his proposed plans for her company. Simone studied them with interest, her eyes nearly popping when she saw some of the figures he'd written down.

But more interesting still was a little doodle he'd done in the corner of one of the pages: a man and a woman holding hands. They were only stick figures, but they were turned to each other and it was easy to interpret them as Cade and herself. She felt quite impressed, until she looked at another sheet and saw the same two figures but with a bold black X through the woman's body.

Her other nightmare scenario returned to haunt her—did it mean that Cade wanted her off the scene? Was that what the cross meant—he was going to annihilate her? Did he intend to take over the company completely, not wanting to be a mere partner, but instead wanting the lot?

Suspicion and anger rose like bile in her throat, and she knew that she couldn't sit here waiting and fuming. She had to talk to someone.

Ros answered at the first ring. 'Simone, I was just thinking about you. You must be telepathic. How're things?'

'I think I've done something very stupid,' confessed Simone.

'And you want to talk? Give me your address and—'

'I can't do that,' insisted Simone hastily.

'Is Cade there?'

'No, but—'

'You're expecting him back any minute. OK, I get the picture. What's your problem?'

It took Simone a moment or two to decide exactly how much to tell Simone. Then, taking a deep breath, she said, 'I think Cade's trying to take my company off me.'

'What?' asked her friend. 'I thought he was helping.'

'So did I, but now I'm not so sure.'

'Surely he can't do that?' demanded Ros ferociously. 'Do you have proof?'

A couple of doodles! Simone suddenly realised how stupid it sounded. 'Nothing concrete,' she admitted lamely.

'Perhaps you're reading the signals wrong. All I'd say is be careful, Simone. There's a lot of history between you two, and it might be difficult to judge exactly what's happening. Don't sign anything until you've triple-read it. Get a lawyer, if necessary. From what I remember, Cade was such a nice guy. Why would he do such a thing?'

'He's after me because he lost all that money. He still doesn't believe I was innocent.'

'Then the man's an idiot,' stated Ros vehemently. 'If it's revenge he's after, then he'll have me to contend with as well. Just watch yourself, Simone. You're far too intelligent to let him walk all over you.'

'Thanks, Ros, but— Oh, he's here. I've just heard the car. Must go.'

Cade looked into Simone's face and knew that all hell was about to break loose. Here was a woman ready for battle. And, contrarily, she had never looked more sexy. Physical need rose to taunt him, putting fire in his belly and hunger in his groin. It was all he could do not to crush her against him and kiss her soundly.

When she had reneged on him earlier he had felt bitter disappointment, anger, even. She'd made a fool of him, and if he hadn't taken himself off he might have done something very unfortunate. Instead his day had been extremely productive. He'd visited his various suppliers, and all the promises they'd made were being upheld. He was very positive about the future where MM Charters were concerned. Less so about Simone.

She was gunning for him. It would appear that she'd spent all day simmering because he'd gone out. Had her pretence of not wanting to make love any longer backfired, and she was blaming him? She was amazingly beautiful in her anger and it was going to be sheer hell keeping his hands off her while she let fly.

He wondered briefly what she was doing in his office. Not that there was anything he didn't want her to see. Perhaps she had hoped to help. Except that, whatever she had been doing, it hadn't put her in a good frame of mind.

'What's wrong?' he asked casually.

Simone's chin came up; every part of her too-attractive body rose to its full height, while her gorgeous violet eyes stabbed into his. 'I want to know, Cade, exactly what your plans for the future are.'

Her question dumbfounded him. Whatever he had expected, it hadn't been this. 'I don't know what you're talking about.' He kept his voice calm, knowing that here was a situation that needed defusing. 'You know what's going on. I've kept nothing back.'

'Haven't you?' Her eyes flared an even darker purple. 'Is it your intention to take over the company completely? Cut me out altogether? Don't take me for a fool, Cade, I won't have it. MM Charters is mine. I'm paying my debt to you by—by living here and being your mistress. It's what we agreed on.'

Cade had no idea where she'd got this idea. Anger flamed in her cheeks, and she looked so staggeringly lovely that he wanted to take her right now, over the desk, on the floor, anywhere so long as he made her his.

But he knew that to do so, even attempt it, would be like a red rag to a bull. Simone would fight like the very devil, and it wouldn't be conducive to seeing this thing through.

'I'm asking nothing more from you,' he said calmly, crushing his desires, banning them to a safe place to be released later when things were different between them. 'I shall hand the company over when my part in it is finished and will simply be a silent partner. Whatever gave you any other idea?'

Simone shook her head, refusing to answer, but the defensive brightness in her eyes remained.

'I thought we'd go out to dinner,' he said in an attempt to change the subject. 'I've booked us a table at—'

'No thanks!' Her refusal was swift and positive.

Cade smiled and deliberately lowered his voice. 'You mean you'd prefer a more intimate meal here?'

He got the exact response he'd expected.

'I don't want to eat with you. I'm not hungry.'

'You've already eaten?'

Simone shook her head.

'Then I insist,' he said. 'We'll eat here, if it will make you any happier, but I'd like you to wear one of your new dresses.'

Simone's eyes flared, but he held her gaze and gave her no chance to back out. In the end she huffed her way out of the room, and although he'd scored a victory Cade somehow didn't feel that he had much to celebrate.

'More wine?'

Simone shook her head. The evening was proving to be every inch the ordeal she had expected. She had almost

flunked out of wearing something Cade had paid for in prefer-
ence for shorts and T-shirt. Cade wasn't her keeper, why
should she do what he asked?

At the last minute common sense had prevailed. It wouldn't
be wise to cross Cade, not at this stage of their relationship—
if it could be called that. It was more like an arrangement
than a relationship, even if he did score highly in the body-
temperature stakes.

She wore a floaty dress in shades of lilac and soft sea-
green, with matching, delicate green sandals on her feet.
Although she hated to admit it, she felt like a million dollars—
she had never worn anything so expensive in her life. It
actually felt a sin to wear it simply to eat dinner out on the
deck. It was a dress made for high society, for dining in the
best restaurants, for a wedding, perhaps. She really ought to
have accepted his invitation to dine out.

Cade never took his eyes off her the whole evening, and
there were moments when she basked in his admiration, when
she felt her heart swell and a very real need to be possessed
by him sweep over her. But there were others when sanity prevailed, when she resented what he was making her do.
Because at the end of the day, no matter what he said, he
intended winning the prize.

And she was not it. She was simply a means to an end. A
very pleasurable means, as far as he was concerned. Simone
mentally shook her head. What had she got herself into? She
had thought Cade was her saviour—instead he was turning
out to be her destroyer.

'You've been very quiet this evening. Is something troubling
you? Guilty conscience, perhaps?'

'Why should I feel guilty?' she cut in swiftly.

'You're surely not forgetting the terms of our contract?'

Simone closed her eyes for a brief second. 'As if you'd ever let me.' She felt uncomfortable as his beautiful eyes grazed over her. She knew what he was thinking, that he wanted to take her to bed, that this fancy evening was nothing more than a prelude to making love.

Fantastic love—she must not forget that. No one could ever say that Cade's love-making didn't warrant full marks.

'You look stunning this evening, Simone. Thank you for dressing up for me.'

'I don't need your thanks,' she retorted coolly. 'It was a command, remember?'

Cade's eyes hardened fractionally. 'Is that how you saw it? It was a suggestion, nothing more.'

'And, if I'd turned up in a pair of frayed shorts and an old T-shirt, what would you have said then?'

'That you still look gorgeous,' came his surprising answer. 'You look lovely in anything you wear, Simone. But tonight there's something extra special about you.'

His eyes roved slowly over her body, lingering on the deep V of the neckline, sending liquid fire through Simone's veins, setting every pulse on high alert. They followed a line down to the throbbing centre of her that she knew he intended to make his own very soon now.

And, Lord help her, she wouldn't be able to stop him.

'Maybe it's the dress, maybe not,' he mused. 'Maybe it's whatever thoughts are going on inside your beautiful head. I used to think that I knew you inside out, Simone, but I was mistaken. I don't know you at all.'

'No more mistaken than I was in thinking that you'd believe in me,' she retorted.

Cade nodded briefly. 'This isn't the time or the place to be talking like this. This is an evening made for lovers.'

The sun had sunk as they dined, and the sky had gone through a whole gamut of colours. It was now making its spectacular final display of violet and crimson, of mulberry and indigo, each tiny cloud on the horizon reflecting the amazing intoxication of colour.

Yes, thought Simone, an evening made for lovers. What a pity they weren't true lovers. What a shame that their relationship was based on punishment and revenge.

Nevertheless her body had been responding to Cade's all evening, and now reached such a fever pitch that she was desperate for him to make love to her. Not that she would ever tell him so—unless he read it in her eyes. She couldn't help wondering whether they revealed her innermost thoughts. He used to say they did. He had said she was like an open book. From the piped music in the house the strains of a waltz could be heard, and Cade got to his feet, holding out his hand. 'Let's dance,' he murmured, his voice softly seductive.

Simone knew that the inevitable was about to happen, that soon he would waltz her away to their bedroom, where a night of incredible passion would make her forget what a devious mind he had.

So, instead of simply slipping into his arms, instead of allowing the moment to embrace her, she put off the inevitable, tugging her hand away from his the second she was on her feet. 'I know I'm supposed to let you do this, I know it's part of the deal.' There was panic in her voice but she didn't hear it. 'But I can't, not any more, I simply can't.' She turned and ran, kicking off her sandals to race along the beach.

She was aware that Cade stood in stunned disbelief for a few seconds, aware that she must have sounded neurotic, but hell, wasn't that what she was? This was a crazy situation. Enough to drive anyone insane.

'Simone, wait!'

Cade's imperious voice reached her and she upped her pace, even though she knew it was futile; Cade's long legs would soon carry him to her. They did, sooner than she'd expected. She heard the scrunching of his feet in the soft sand getting closer and closer, and without even turning she knew when he had caught up.

Abruptly she stopped and turned, and he almost cannoned into her. She expected anger, she expected a volley of words denouncing her actions. Instead he pulled her heaving body against his and found the softness of her lips with his own.

The hardness of him—his chest rising and falling in unison, the pressure of his mouth, the sweet, sweet sensation he managed to induce—served to send every harsh thought spinning into the air, to be instantly replaced by naked hunger.

It was as though her run had whipped up her emotions to fever pitch and she drank from his mouth, eager to taste, to take, to receive, to respond. She wanted to let him know how she felt. She wanted him to…

Cade needed no telling, no encouragement. A guttural groan came from deep in his throat, and the pressure of his mouth increased . He took what she gave but demanded no more.

Simone pressed into him, revelling in his arousal, aware that he must be struggling to contain himself. An impish desire to play made her wriggle out of his arms and run again, this time towards the ocean. With no thought for the expensive dress, she waded into the water, glancing over her shoulder to check that Cade was pursuing her.

What followed was a cat-and-mouse game. Each time

he caught up with her she fled again. Finally, he caught her and brought her to the ground. They rolled in the shallows, Simone laughing and crying out until his mouth silenced her. It claimed her more potently than ever before, drinking from her, telling her without the need for words what he intended to do.

CHAPTER EIGHT

'I THOUGHT we'd go into Airlie Beach today,' announced Cade.

A whole week had passed since Simone had ruined her expensive dress. A week where not much had mattered apart from the passion that pulsed between them. There had been times when Simone felt as though they were on honeymoon, so close was the bond between them.

Something deep down inside her—not rationale, that was for sure—told her that since she was in a no-win situation she might as well take pleasure in her time spent with Cade. But 'much wanted more', went the old saying, and Simone wanted more of this gorgeous man. She wanted him at her side for the rest of her life.

Knowing that this would never happen sometimes made her wish that she hadn't got involved again. He was her one true love, and when they ultimately parted she would be beside herself. Even knowing what his game was made no difference. Her mind might know the desolation and devastation that lay ahead, but her heart didn't. Her heart was hell-bent on enjoying itself.

'I'd like that,' she said. 'I need to shop.'

Cade frowned. 'For what? Don't you have all you need here?'

Fresh food was delivered daily, and Simone's wardrobe

was now more than adequate. In fact she had clothes that she felt sure she would never wear. 'Toiletries,' she announced. 'Things you can't buy for me.' Though she was inclined to think that he wished he could. If she let him, he would take over her whole life.

Isn't he doing that already? asked a tiny voice inside her head. Simone chose to ignore it. Of course he wasn't. She would never allow it. He was simply doing her a big favour by rebuilding her company.

Later when they stopped in front of the offices of MM Charters Simone gasped. 'Wow!' Her entire office block had been extended and given a face lift.

'Surprised?' asked Cade with an amused lift of one brow.

There was an easy camaraderie between them—no one could fail to notice that they were lovers. It was written all over their faces, it was expressed in their body language, and even if Simone felt that she was hiding her feelings nothing could be further from the truth.

'Surprised doesn't begin to express how I feel,' she said, smiling up into his face. 'How have you achieved so much in such a short space of time?'

Cade shrugged.

'Money talks, is that it?' she asked, unable to stop a faint hint of cynicism entering her voice.

Cade let it pass. 'It helps,' he admitted. 'Though I believe in a fair price for a fair job. I pay no one over the odds.'

Simone wondered what her final price would be. How much would Cade demand in return for the wonders he had worked?

When Cade ushered her through the door into her old office Simone could see that a dramatic transformation had continued inside too. There were now three offices instead of two, but at the moment they stood empty. 'Why three offices?' she asked, still suspecting that Cade might want to be more involved when this thing was over.

'I thought you could do with the space, it's as simple as that,' he said, and the look in his eyes suggested that he knew exactly what she was thinking. 'With a bigger fleet you'll need extra staff.'

And with that she had to be satisfied.

'I need to talk to the builders,' said Cade a few minutes later. 'I'll meet you in the coffee shop around the corner in, say, half an hour. Will that give you time?'

Simone's eyes flared. 'What have you got to say to them that you don't want me to hear?'

Cade merely smiled, bowing his head to drop a kiss to her brow. 'What a suspicious mind you have. You can stay if you like, but it will be boring talk, I assure you. It's just a few minor details, nothing to worry your pretty head about.'

His golden eyes held hers for several pulse-racing seconds, and Simone's anger dissolved, as he had known it would. She wanted to stay, she wanted to be in on everything. She hated herself for being weak, but when he looked at her like that how could she help it? At least she knew he was doing a good job, and she had to trust that he had the business's best interests at heart.

'Half an hour, then,' she said softly. 'Not a minute longer.' She gave him a lingering look as he headed towards the band of men outside.

Simone had been sitting in the welcome relief of the air-conditioned café for less than a minute when a hand touched her shoulder. Thinking it was Cade, her heart lurched, as it had done a hundred times a day for the last however-how-long—she was beginning to lose count. She turned with a smile, only to have it wiped off her face. 'Gerard!' Her ex-husband was the last man in the world she'd expected to see.

'Now there's a welcome. You haven't seen me for over a year, and that's all you can say?'

'I thought you'd left the area.' Simone kept her voice harsh, her eyes flashing her disapproval, making no attempt to hide her hostility.

'I did,' he answered. 'But now I'm back.' He looked at the empty table in front of her. 'You haven't ordered yet? Allow me. What would you like—iced tea? Is it still your favourite?'

'I'm expecting company,' she told him bluntly. And even if she wasn't she would have lied simply to get rid of him. He had no part to play in her life any more, and she was finding it difficult to be civil.

Blond brows rose. 'Anyone I know?'

'It's none of your business,' she retorted, her voice crisp and unwelcoming.

Gerard seemed not to notice. Either that or he ignored it. 'Perhaps I'd like to make it mine,' he said, sitting down opposite, his eyes steady on hers. 'What's going on?'

'Excuse me, I said I was meeting someone,' she flared, anger making her eyes turn deep purple. 'You and I have nothing to say to each other. Please go.'

But Gerard totally disregarded her request, smiling instead, not taking his eyes off her. 'You look stunning. Ravishing, in fact. It's my guess there's a new man in your life.'

'That's none of your business either,' she rejoined fiercely.

'I'd like to make it mine,' he announced, his voice deeply meaningful. 'It was a mistake divorcing you, Simone.' He tried to take her hand across the table, looking hurt when she snatched it away. 'We should have tried harder.'

Simone's eyes flashed her disgust. 'I wasn't the one to go

off with someone else. What did you expect me to do—wait around until you'd had your fling? No chance, Gerry. You did the unforgivable.'

'At least let me buy you a drink.'

Gerard had a thatch of blond hair and eyes the colour of a pale sky. He was of medium height with broad shoulders and, looking at him now, Simone wondered what she had ever seen in him. He had none of the charisma of Cade, that was for sure, and she had no intention of being nice to him. 'No thanks,' she said tightly. 'Like I said, I'm meeting someone.'

His lips thinned but he didn't take the hint and go away. 'I couldn't help noticing,' he said instead, 'how much work is being done over at your office. Have you sold the company? I'm sure you don't have that sort of money—unless you've come into a fortune?' His brows rose, and his pale eyes remained steady on hers.

'I have a benefactor,' she admitted, knowing that it would be pointless lying. Everyone knew everyone's business around here. She was probably the talk of the town. Maybe even Gerard knew but wanted to hear it from her own lips.

'Someone I know?'

'Yes, Cade.' It was a defiant answer, her eyes blazing into his, waiting to see what he made of it.

Gerard's shocked face told her that he hadn't heard this piece of news. 'Cade Dupont? Are you crazy or what?'

Gerard didn't know the whole story. He thought they'd simply fallen out. It was bad enough that people knew her father was a drunk and a gambler, without them knowing he had conned Cade out of his inheritance.

Gerard shook his head. 'It's suicidal hooking up with him again. Why's he helping you? What's he after?'

'Why do you care, Gerry?' Simone returned sharply. 'What I do is my own affair.'

Gerard's eyes were derisive. 'No man would invest such a huge amount of money for no return. He's either conning you, Simone, or there's something you're not telling me.'

When she continued to sit in tight-lipped silence he added, 'He's not actually doing this for nothing, is he? It's not his way.'

Simone felt her cheeks grow warm at the thought of her ex deducing what was going on. Gerard would have a field day if he knew she was selling her body for mercenary reasons.

'My assumption is,' he said, his pale eyes watching her face carefully, 'that he wants to take over your company. He's probably suggested that you become partners, but if my intuition is correct he's planning to take it off you. You need to watch your back, Simone.'

'You're wide of the mark,' she claimed, relieved that he hadn't hit on the truth about their relationship, but more than a little disturbed that Gerard too thought Cade was out to rip her off.

'I don't think so,' he asserted. 'And I hope you're not going to let him. Not my feisty Simone. I have first-hand experience of your temper, don't forget. You're not the type to be put upon.'

'And if you don't leave right now you'll see that my temper hasn't improved,' she thrust back wildly.

He glanced at his watch. 'Actually, I do have to go. But I'm glad that I've bumped into you again, and if you should need any back-up give me a call. I'm still on the same number.'

As if she would need his help, thought Simone as he disappeared out of sight. Gerard was the last person she would turn to. The gall of the man, to even think that she'd be interested in him again.

So deep was she in thought that it seemed like only seconds before Cade put in an appearance. In reality it had been almost ten minutes, but Simone's mind was so troubled by Gerard's intrusion that she had been in a world of her own.

She actually jumped when Cade spoke her name.

'Where were you?' he asked, his smile deeply disturbing. It was always this way with Cade; one look out of those golden eyes and she was lost. They crinkled so beautifully at the corners, became almost slumberous, as though he was imagining them in bed together. At the very least they gave her the impression that she was his.

Serious sensations slinked through her body. 'Miles away,' she admitted. She didn't want to tell him about seeing Gerard; it could lead to all sorts of questions.

'Wondering how long I'd be?'

'Mmm,' she agreed. 'I've been sitting here ages.' In fact, she'd ordered a coffee but she hadn't drunk it. It sat in front of her now, an unsavoury skin forming on the top. Cade signalled for fresh drinks and sat down in the chair Gerard had vacated. What a difference in the two men, thought Simone. Cade was a tall, striking figure—the female staff behind the counter couldn't take their eyes off him—whereas Gerard hadn't drawn a second glance even though he was moderately good-looking.

It wasn't the looks that did it. Cade exuded power. He didn't have to say a word or even do anything, people instinctively knew that he was a man used to commanding respect.

'You're very quiet,' commented Cade. 'Is something wrong? Were you missing me?' His voice dropped into seduction mode, and eyes the colour of molten amber burned into hers.

This was crazy, thought Simone, tightening muscles in an effort to shut out the sudden feelings that sprang into vigorous life. It was nothing more than Cade's cunning way of taking her mind off what he was doing to her company. Why else would he have got rid of her while he had talked to the builders? Suddenly Simone couldn't altogether dismiss what Gerard had said about Cade wanting to take over her business, especially when it coincided with her own recent feelings on the matter.

'I was wondering what you were up to with the business,' she answered crisply. 'I'm just a bit uneasy, especially when I let you dismiss me the way you did just now. I must need my head examining. I seem to be letting you run things without me, and I'm not sure why.'

'Because you know my business sense is better than yours,' he answered with a smile designed to melt every hostile thought in her head.

But it didn't work. Not this time. 'I appreciate what you're doing, more than you'll ever know,' she said, her eyes steady on his. 'But it's still my company, Cade, and as such I should be consulted.'

She ought to have put her foot down far earlier instead of that one pathetic attempt she'd made. The trouble was, until now Cade had taken over her mind and body in such a sensational way that she hadn't been able to think clearly. This had undoubtedly been his intention, and she ought to have been aware of it. Instead she'd let herself get carried along on a tide of high emotion.

But not any more. Bumping into Gerard and hearing his take on the subject had opened her eyes. Very wide! If she had nothing else to thank him for, it was this.

Cade's brows rose questioningly. 'I was under the impression that you were willing for me to do whatever was best for the company. What's happened to make you change your mind?'

'I've had time to sit and think,' she declared, 'and I've realised what a fool I'm being.' Simone flashed sharply violet eyes, her body stiff with resentment. 'I've let you seduce me with soft words and a fantastic lifestyle, but I have no idea what's going on. For all I know, you could be planning to take the business from under my feet.'

Simone heard the air being sucked in between Cade's teeth, his eyes, changing to a hard glass-like substance, piercing her with the intensity of a stiletto. 'Where the hell has that come from? Who've you been talking to?'

'So there is something going on?' she countered, knowing that if there wasn't he would have denied it. Cade looked at her long and hard, and Simone felt none of the usual electrifying emotions. She felt nothing now except stone-cold anger. 'I put my trust in you, Cade.'

'You weren't averse to accepting my offer of help, even with its unusual conditions. You knew what to expect, Simone.'

'There is help and there is help!' she retorted. 'Yours is turning into the kind I can do without.'

'So, pray tell me, where has this ridiculous notion come from?' His eyes were as equally glacial as hers now, his whole body rejecting her accusation. 'We've been apart for less than an hour and you've suddenly decided that I'm not your saviour after all. Why?'

'Because you keep things from me.' Simone held his gaze, challenging him to deny it.

'I'm trying to protect you, Simone. You've had a hard time, I thought that—'

'What you thought was that you could twist me round your little finger,' she flared. 'Well, not any more, Cade.'

Cade found it hard to believe that this was the same Simone who shared his bed, who willingly gave her body to his. She had changed from a fiery lover to a fierce opponent in a matter of minutes, and he didn't know why.

'Whoever put this notion into your head has to be seriously insane,' he declared. There had to be someone; she wouldn't have changed like this in such a short space of time. He had taken great delight in keeping her ready for him at all times. And it had worked—until now. She had never been more remote.

'Why should it be anyone?' she countered. 'I came to my senses. I suddenly realised what you were really doing.'

'You mean you put two and two together and made five. You're seriously out of your mind, Simone. You're letting your imagination run away with you. Why would I want to take your business from you?' He could not for the life of him understand where she was coming from.

'Because you wanted to set up here yourself and there were no opportunities—except me! I can't believe I was so gullible. I really thought you wanted to help.'

'And now you think I'm planning to take everything off you?' Even though he had wanted to settle a score, he found it difficult to accept that Simone felt this way. He had half a mind to do exactly what she was accusing him of.

Astonishingly, her flashing amethyst eyes had never made him feel more like taking her to bed. Anger added a whole new dimension, and his body reacted more strongly than he would have liked it to. Nevertheless it was unthinkable. His nostrils flared instead, and he looked at her coldly.

'So where do we go from here?' he asked coldly, pushing himself up from the table. 'Do you want to continue with our deal, or are you backing out?' He saw the sudden uncertainty in her eyes. 'I thought as much. You're not really sure what you're up against, are you, Simone?' He held her gaze for a few seconds before saying, 'It's up to you. I'm going home. You can decide to join me or not.' He threw a handful of coins down on the table and looked pointedly at her.

Simone tossed her hair back from her face and glared at him beautifully. 'Not yet.' And she watched until he had gone from sight.

She was furious with Cade and with herself. She couldn't go back to the beach house—not yet. In fact she had half a mind never to return, but to go back to her family home instead. Except that would mean she would certainly forfeit her business, and would have to face her father, who would gloat at her downfall—and that might be even worse than facing Cade.

There was one person, though, who would listen and put things into perspective. That was her mother. Although Simone hadn't been to see her since Cade had come on the scene, she had phoned every day. She had told her mother that Cade was simply investing in the business and that they were purely business partners. She hadn't informed her mother of the extent of the trouble the business faced, or of her true feelings for Cade. Simone had kept those secret and was now glad that she had.

She took a taxi and picked up her own car, which still sat outside her father's house where she had left it what seemed like a lifetime ago. Simone was faintly surprised that he hadn't sold it in a fit of anger, and thankful that he wasn't at home.

'Simone!' Pamela Maxwell greeted her daughter joyfully. 'What a lovely surprise, I'm so pleased to see you.' Her hug was warm and tight, as though she never wanted to let Simone go, making Simone feel guilty for not coming sooner. 'Have you brought Cade to see me?'

She was sitting in a beautiful, large air-conditioned room with views over gardens that were tended with loving care. There was a fountain to one side, and a pool filled with carp to the other, as well as many beautiful shrubs. Pamela spent many hours in this room. When the weather was cooler she would go outdoors, but today it was almost a hundred degrees and certainly not conducive to sitting outside.

Simone shook her head. 'No, Mum. I'm afraid we've had a falling out.'

'Oh dear,' said her mother. 'What does that mean for the business?'

The business—of course, thought Simone ungraciously. It was still her mother's first love. That was natural enough, but she would have preferred her mother to be more concerned for her daughter's feelings. 'I'm sure the business will be fine, Mum. I've not actually walked out on him,' she said. 'But, oh, I don't know. I'm totally confused.'

Her mother smiled comfortingly. 'Suppose you tell me about it. I'll ring for some tea, shall I?' A cup of tea was her mother's remedy for all ills. 'By the way, how's your father?'

'Have you seen him?' asked Simone.

Pamela shook her head. 'He never even phones.'

'I'm sorry, Mum.'

'It's not your fault. He's a silly old coot. He'll drink himself to death, you know.'

Pamela Maxwell was still a good-looking woman. She took care over her appearance. Her iron-grey hair was neatly combed, her favourite mauve dress was clean and crease-free. She wore her much-loved pearl earrings that her husband had given her on their wedding day. She was gracious in her illness, and Simone loved her to death.

'I haven't seen him either,' she admitted. 'Not since I moved in with Cade.'

'Cade, yes,' said her mother, her pale lavender eyes lighting up. 'Tell me again how it all came about. I was most surprised when you said he was back in Australia.'

No more surprised than Simone had been. 'We bumped into each other in a restaurant. We got chatting, and he said that he was interested in finding an investment in the area. I thought the business could do with a bit of a boost, and we agreed a suitable plan for both of us.' Simone still didn't have the heart to tell her mother how close she had been to losing the business.

'I always knew he was a good man,' nodded Pamela. 'When I found out your father had stolen that money, I could have killed him. I was so sorry when Cade left the country, and I'm pleased that he's back. But, tell me, why have you fallen out?'

Simone grimaced. 'I think he's planning to take the business off me.'

Her mother's eyes widened and she sat up a bit straighter. 'What? He can't do that, can he? Has he said as much?'

'No,' admitted Simone. 'But Cade's so secretive about what he's doing, he never involves me. Don't you think I have reason to be suspicious?'

'Have you asked him outright?'

Simone nodded.

'Did he deny it?'

'Not exactly. He was indignant that I should even think it, but then he skirted the subject. I don't know what to believe.'

'I think,' said her mother, 'that the two of you need to talk. My money's on Cade being honourable. On the other hand,' she admitted, pursing her lips ruefully, 'he does have good reason to get his own back.'

'Thanks, Mum,' said Simone with a laugh. 'I knew I could count on you.'

After that their conversation turned to more mundane things. When she finally left the nursing home, Simone was feeling much better. Her mother had managed to put Simone's mind at rest, and Simone was feeling more convinced that Cade had no plans to steal her business. He had stuck to his side of the bargain so far, and Simone just had to trust that he would hand over the company to her when their arrangement came to an end. Her mother had suggested that the next time Simone visited she bring him with her. 'I'd love to see Cade again,' she said. 'There is a lot I'd like to talk to him about.'

CHAPTER NINE

'IT'S UP to you whether you believe me.' Simone faced Cade over dinner on the outdoor deck, not happy that he didn't accept she'd been to see her mother. He had been waiting for her when she got home, his face as black as thunder, and she couldn't help wondering why he was so angry.

He acted as though she belonged to him. She was obligated, yes, she owed him big-time, but surely she still had the right to a life of her own? He couldn't command every second of her day.

'You have no reason to lie, I agree,' he admitted, picking up his wine glass and calmly taking a sip. 'But even so it seems strange that you suddenly shot off to see your mother without telling me.'

'Do you own me?' she demanded recklessly, feeling like knocking the glass right out of his hand. 'I know you'd like to, but the truth is that you don't. We have an agreement that I be your mistress until the business is back on its feet, but there's nothing to say that I can't go and see my mother—or whomever else I want to see, for that matter.'

Cade's eyes were dark and grim. 'Regardless of what you say, Simone, something happened to you today even before you visited your parent.' Cade had sat alone for a long time after their earlier argument. He had thought Simone would follow him obediently back to the beach house and beg his forgiveness. In truth it had shocked him when she hadn't, and he had spent the past hours pacing and awaiting her return. For a moment he had feared that she might never return.

'If you don't believe me, Cade, call her,' insisted Simone at once. 'She'll verify my story.'

But Cade shook his head. 'That's not necessary. I think we should get on with our meal and forget it,' he decided, slanting her a darkly condemning glance. He desperately wanted things to go back to normal between them. He wanted to taste her lips, and experience that fiery passion of hers between the sheets.

'Perhaps you can forget it,' she mocked, 'but it's not so easy for me, being on the receiving end. In fact, I'm not hungry.' She scraped back her chair and fled indoors, racing to the bedroom and banging the door so violently that it was in danger of falling off its hinges.

Once there, she threw herself down on the bed, lying flat on her back staring at the ceiling, her fingers curled into fists at her side. It took her a long time to relax and calm down. During her reflective moment, she thought back to her conversations with Gerard and her mother. Both had mentioned the troubled past between her and Cade, and Simone grudgingly accepted that perhaps Cade did have a reason for his behaviour. As far as he was concerned, she had lied to him about her father's business. Once a liar, always a liar—wasn't that what they said? She was branded whether she liked it or not.

Simone was asleep when Cade finally came to bed, curled up on top of the luxurious silken sheets, still fully dressed. She stirred when she felt him easing off her top but drugged by sleep, she forgot what had happened earlier and curved her arms around his neck, drinking in the exciting male smell of him, bringing his face down for a kiss.

Cade groaned deep in his throat and captured her mouth with fierce lips. Not a word was spoken as he drank in the sweet heat of her desire, and it was not long before the kiss exploded in a fury of tangled arms and limbs, of nibbling, biting teeth, and eager, exploring hands.

Rockets went off inside Simone's head, exploding sensationally as Cade took first one of her hard stinging nipples into his mouth and then the other, nipping and teasing, making her mindless with screaming pleasure. Her senses throbbed and her mind floated as his hands touched and tormented each part of her body in turn.

Everything was forgotten except mind-dazzling sensations, and heated spirals of desire that threatened to rocket her to the highest heavens. When he dragged down her briefs, when his knowledgeable fingers touched and teased the places that only he knew best, Simone felt every one of her muscles tensing in agony and ecstasy.

At the same time his mouth drugged what little was left of her senses, demanding and persuading, as if she needed any persuasion! Cade had reduced her to a wanton woman, to someone who wanted nothing but release from the torture he was putting her through.

'Cade.' She clutched her hands round the back of his neck. 'Cade, take me, please, now. I can't wait any longer.'

He lifted his head and she saw darkly golden eyes that were full of the same greed and need that ravaged her. He trailed fingers down her cheek, hovering over her lips, then followed a further line down her throat and over her breasts. Simone squirmed in an agony of tightly suppressed desires, reaching her arms up and around him, pulling him down hard on her, forcing him to do as she asked.

She hooked her legs around him and arched her body, and then went wild in a matter of seconds. That was all it took to make her pulse and explode with sheer unadulterated pleasure. Never had it been so good. Never had he managed to arouse her in so many different ways all at the same time.

And then it was Cade's turn to experience a deep, shuddering heat that rocked his body and threw him into orbit. He held her so tight that it hurt. He kissed her again and again, neither of them wanting this utterly magical moment to end.

Nor did it.

As soon as their body heat lowered, as soon as their breathing returned to normal, he started again, only this time he took it more slowly. He touched, he stroked, he teased. He kissed gently and looked at her with burning eyes. The question was unspoken when he entered her again. It was a mutual acceptance, grown of familiarity and a knowledge that they needed each other.

And like that, curved into each other, they went to sleep. It was not until she woke to find the first pale fingers of dawn streaking the sky, to discover Cade's seriously sexy body up close to hers, that Simone realised what had happened. What she didn't know was whether he had taken her in the heat of anger or whether his need had been as seriously hungry as her own.

Whichever, the outcome had made her forget her anger. Cade's love-making had carried her into a far-off world where nothing mattered except burning senses and scorching passion, where blood pounded and hearts galloped, where two bodies met and became one.

Even thinking about it brought a fresh surge of hunger, and

while Cade lay asleep she trailed lazy fingers over his bronze chest, tracing the whorls of dark hair, the magnificent muscles, feeling the light rise and fall of his breathing. She pushed herself up on one elbow and began dropping light kisses on to his skin, the musky smell of him so intoxicating that she grew bolder and slicked her tongue over his hard, tight nipples, grazing them with her even white teeth.

He tasted good, so good that she got carried away, and her hand slid beneath the satin sheet draped over his hips to discover that even in his sleep Cade was excitingly aroused. She simply had to touch, to hold, to stroke...

At what time Cade awoke Simone didn't know, but when she glanced at his face she was alarmed to see that his eyes were open. Narrow golden slits were watching every movement she made. What must he be thinking? she wondered.

He would know that he had her exactly where he wanted her, came the swift answer.

With a shake of her head she rolled back into the space beside him. Her next move was to slide off the bed, but Cade's arm fell heavily across her. 'Why stop now?' he asked in a voice still thick with sleep.

Such a gloriously sexy voice! It sent tingles from the top of her head to the soles of her feet. Her whole body trembled. 'I didn't know you were awake,' she whispered.

'Which made it all the more exciting, my brave little one. Let's pretend I'm still asleep.' He lowered his lids over eyes that were too hot for Simone's peace of mind.

She couldn't touch him now, not knowing that he was aware of the need sizzling inside her. She wasn't used to taking the lead; she'd only done it because she'd thought he was asleep.

When nothing happened, when Simone didn't move an

inch, a groan came from deep in Cade's throat, and the next thing she knew he had hauled her on top of him. 'Ride me,' he urged in his rich, deep voice. 'Take what you desperately need.'

Their eyes met and locked and Simone felt his power flow into her, and suddenly she was shy no longer. She eased herself over him, and marvelled at this rawness of feeling that empowered her.

In that moment she knew that she loved this man more than life itself. It wasn't about sex, or need, or hunger. It went far deeper than that. When their deal was over, when he disappeared from her life again, she would want to sink into a hole in the ground and die. The thought of life without Cade was sheer hell.

She wasn't even aware that tears squeezed from her eyes and began to slide down her cheeks, she was conscious only of being in the unique position of dominating Cade. Feeling him under her and inside her, feeling him buck with the same sort of intense hunger, feeling his hands behind her hips urging her on, threw her mind into disarray. And when suddenly their positions were reversed, when Cade rolled her over so that he could take the lead, she stopped thinking and gave herself up to the powerful sensations that ripped through her body.

It was almost lunchtime before they finally made it out of the bedroom. Simone had never felt so gloriously alive. Every inch of her body sizzled. Such fantastic feelings. She felt as though she was walking on air. She felt like the most loved woman in the world, and refused to let herself think any differently.

She realised in that moment that perhaps she was doing Cade an injustice. Surely he wouldn't treat her as though she were his most precious possession if he didn't feel something more for her than just lust? Surely he wasn't contemplating taking the business off her?

Perhaps her mother was right—she really ought to learn to trust Cade, to take his word. After all, she had no real proof to the contrary. There was nothing except the demons in her own mind, and the uneasiness she felt at the thought of Cade leaving her again.

It would be wiser to stop believing that Cade was out to swindle her, to be grateful for all that he was doing, and enjoy their fantastic love life.

Even thinking about it caused her heart to leap into life, and every pulse to race until they were out of sorts with themselves. Surely she wouldn't feel like this if she were certain that Cade was out to dupe her? She wouldn't even want him to touch her. Instead all she could dream about was his kisses, his—

'We'll take the yacht over to one of the islands.' Cade's voice broke into her thoughts. 'If you pack a picnic, I'll get it ready. And find something to nibble on the way, I'm starving.' Then his voice became low and sexy. 'I need sustenance to keep up with you.'

Simone was about to toss back some smart remark when she realised that he was joking. 'It takes two to tango,' she quipped.

He nodded briefly. 'We make quite a team, you and me, don't we?'

Simone nodded, resolutely pushing away the last of her doubts. 'I'll go and see what we've got to eat.'

Cade hummed to himself as he made a thorough check of the yacht. He still felt that Simone was hiding something, and he had every intention of finding out what it was. But it would wait. The way she had initiated their love-making this morning suggested that finding out wouldn't be difficult—so long as he didn't lose his temper again! Which might prove tricky if she insisted on being secretive.

He was damn sure something had happened to make her think that he wanted to claim the business for himself. She'd said she wanted to do some shopping, but he'd felt that was a lie right from the beginning. Had she actually had a secret assignation? Was there a spy in the camp who was feeding her mind with all sorts of stories?

What he did know was that he didn't intend to let her out of his sight in future. His plans for revenge were being thwarted, and he wasn't happy about it. He didn't want the company, he wanted—

No, he didn't want to think about what he wanted too much. Best just to stick to his original plan. He'd told Simone that he'd become her partner in return for her sharing his bed, and he had no intention of going back on his word. It wasn't his objective to fleece her, even though she'd had no compunction about ripping him off. All he wanted was to make her feel as though her world had come to an end when he walked out at the end of the day.

That was where her punishment would lie.

He'd planned to make her fall in love with him all over again, and until yesterday morning he'd thought he was well on the way. She was quite an actress, because even after their fight last night she hadn't been averse to him making love to her. In fact their love-making had never been so intense.

So why did it worry him rather than please him?

'Hey, what are you thinking about?' Cade called down to Simone where she sat on the deck, staring into space. They'd been on their journey for almost an hour, nibbling on fruit and cheese and crackers, drinking coffee and orange juice as though their dry throats could never be quenched. Although on the surface there was no tension between them, it simmered beneath like a pot about to boil over.

'Nothing,' came the disappointing answer. 'I'm watching the waves.'

Liar, he thought. She was somewhere else, in a world that he was not allowed to inhabit. Perhaps he was wasting his time and she would never fall in love with him again. Perhaps her fertile imagination had worked things out and she was already feeling deep disappointment.

Cade shook his head. Simone had become an enigma. 'Come up here with me,' he said, holding out his hand invitingly.

It was with such reluctance that she did so that he began to question the reason she had amazingly seduced him this morning. She had never run this hot and cold before. 'Do you want to steer?' he asked when she joined him. As on the previous occasion he had chosen to use the engine rather than sail, believing it would give him more time to lavish on Simone.

She shook her head.

'Care to tell me what's troubling you—apart from the fact that you think I'm about to renege on our deal?' he asked, hearing a hint of cynicism in his voice. He cursed beneath his breath. He didn't want to antagonise her, it was just that he was so damn angry about the whole thing.

'I—I don't think that any more,' she answered quietly, looking up at him with her huge eyes.

Cade felt his heart stop. 'What did you say?'

'I—I'm doing my best to trust you.'

He could see how hard it was for her to say these words and, throwing caution to the winds, he dragged her into his arms. 'You've no idea how much it means to me to hear you say that.' Although he kept his voice low and calm, privately he was leaping with joy. Whatever had happened to make her change her mind, he was truly grateful. This is what he had planned all along, but his victory was even more rewarding than he had hoped.

Several long minutes passed before he felt Simone gradually relax against him. He pressed a tiny kiss to her forehead, steering with one hand while holding her with the other. 'No more harsh thoughts?'

'No,' she whispered, and amazingly she lifted her head and offered her mouth.

Simone knew that she was being seduced by the magic of the moment, which included not only Cade's excitingly sexy body close to hers but the whole enchantment of their surroundings. The ocean was inclined to be a little choppy, with a south-easterly breeze, but it didn't bother her in the least. In fact, she embraced it when she was thrust even closer against Cade.

In the distance she could see their destination getting closer, and conversely now she didn't want to reach the island; she wanted to stay here with Cade. She didn't want any intrusion on their privacy. Odd, when only last night she'd been protesting that she had the right to see whomever she liked.

It was amazing what coupling their bodies in fierce lovemaking had done. It had got rid of all her doubts. She wanted nothing more than to be with Cade, only Cade, experiencing the excitement of simply looking at him. He was so gorgeously, gorgeously sexy. Not that sex was the be all and end all of life, but at this moment in time it played a major impact on her senses.

His kiss was deep and drugging, it swallowed up everything inside her, convincing her that her bones had liquefied, and if he let her go she would pool at his feet. He kept her at his side until they reached land, and as soon as he'd anchored he led her down to the master stateroom.

'Cade,' she protested mildly. 'We shouldn't be doing this again.' The throbbing heart of her wanted him desperately, but there was a part of her that was afraid she was giving too much of herself away.

'Why?' he asked teasingly. 'Getting fed up of me?'

'No, never,' she answered with humiliating quickness.

'Good.' That one word was spoken in a gloriously deep and meaningful voice, his eyes razoring her skin as though he were actually touching her.

In her heightened state, Simone's senses took over. It was sheer insanity, but there was not a thing she could do about it. Her legs were hollow, her heart on fire, and letting Cade make love to her yet again sounded like heaven on earth. Which it was! They spent so much time playing love games and then renewing their energy by sleep that they never actually got off the boat.

Soon it was early evening and they were on deck sipping champagne, dipping strawberries into melted chocolate and feeding each other. 'I suggest we stay here overnight,' said Cade, his golden eyes never leaving hers.

Unaware that her face was that of a woman who had well and truly been made-love to—her eyes glowing like two soft orbs of ethereal light, her lips plump and soft and even more inviting than before—Simone smiled. 'Whatever you want, Cade.'

It was the triumphant gleam in his eyes that did it. The gleam that told her she'd been brought to her knees. He'd seduced her into believing that she was in love with him, into believing that her whole future was going to be rosy. She'd spent so many hours in his arms and in his bed that she'd been sucked into his universe.

Whatever you want, Cade!

How stupid was that? It made her sound like a love-struck teenager. Her eyes flared a dangerous purple. 'Actually, no, Cade. I'd prefer to go home.' Her voice was all at once tight and cool, with no hint of the languid warmth she had felt a few seconds earlier. And when she said 'home' she didn't mean his rented beach-house, though she had no intention of telling him that until they got there.

Dark brows rose. 'What's brought about this sudden change of heart?'

'Nothing.'

But of course he knew there was something wrong. Cade could read her like a book. He knew almost every thought that went through her head.

'Don't lie to me, Simone,' he said crisply. 'Some dark force has just entered your mind. I want to know what it is.'

'I don't have to tell you anything,' she rejoined, her eyes not wavering for one second from his. Even as she spoke Simone got to her feet and fled to the steps leading down to the galley.

The next thing Cade heard was a loud cry and a thud.

And then silence.

CHAPTER TEN

SIMONE regained consciousness to feel her head cradled between a pair of firm, warm hands. Through a mist she saw concerned golden eyes looking into hers, and from a long way away she heard a deep voice ask whether she was all right.

'Simone, speak to me,' said the voice more urgently.

Simone opened her mouth and tried to say something, but all she could hear was a strange distorted whisper that sounded nothing like her normally well-modulated voice. She licked lips that were bone dry and tried to swallow.

'Simone, can you hear me?'

'Yes.' This time she managed a faint sound, and as her vision cleared she saw relief flood Cade's face.

'Does anywhere hurt?'

'No.' In fact she felt strangely comfortable, especially with Cade looking down at her with the oddest of expressions. As though he really cared. Which had to be a figment of her imagination. He cared only that she had hurt herself, not in any other way. She mustn't even dare to think that.

'Then let me help you up.' One firm hand slid beneath her neck, another beneath her back to ease her into a sitting position. But the instant he took her arm to help her stand, the instant she put pressure on her foot, she yelped out in pain. 'I think I've twisted my ankle,' she acknowledged with a wry grimace.

Without hesitation Cade swung her up into his arms.

Held closely against him, Simone could feel the exciting pump of his heart, the electrifying warmth of his skin, and although her ankle was hurting like hell she was more aware of Cade's drugging maleness. She snuggled her head into his shoulder, secretly inhaling his intoxicating smell—fresh air, ocean spray, even a little of her own perfume, but above all the raw, animal scent of him.

Was it crazy or what? She couldn't help herself. Her mind soared into dizzying space, and when he eventually put her down on the oversized bed they had already made good use of she felt oddly bereft. Cheated, even, even though her ankle was beginning to swell and the pain was becoming more intense.

'You'll be OK while I fetch some ice?' he enquired gently.

When Simone nodded she discovered that her head hurt as well. Her eyes creased with pain, and she put up her hand and found a lump.

Instantly Cade took a look and his frown worried her.

'What can you see?'

'A slight abrasion,' he answered gruffly. 'Already swelling.'

He was back in no time with a bag of crushed ice wrapped in a tea towel, which he folded around her ankle. He'd also brought a glass of water, which he held to her lips as though she wasn't capable of holding it for herself. Another ice pack was pressed to her head.

Cade thought that Simone might need to see a doctor, and he debated whether to find one here on the island or take the boat back to the mainland. Finally, after an inner struggle, and as her injuries weren't life threatening, he decided on the latter—except that by now it was dark and he knew it would be madness to attempt the journey.

During the night, however, Simone became hot and agitated, and he blamed himself for believing that she'd be OK until they got home. 'I'm going to fetch a doctor,' he told her hoarsely. 'I won't be long. Don't move, whatever you do, don't attempt to get out of bed.'

He managed to locate a physician who agreed to come out to the yacht, and after a thorough examination the man didn't seem unduly worried. 'I suggest you stay right here in bed, young lady, until you get home—and then go to see your own doctor, especially if you become confused. I don't think you have concussion, but best keep an eye on it. And have that ankle x-rayed. It's difficult to judge whether you've torn any ligaments since it's so swollen.'

Cade never closed his eyes. He sat in a chair, watching Simone sleep, conscious of her head injury. He felt responsible. Somehow his suggestion that they stay on the yacht overnight had spooked her. Why else had she sprinted for the galley?

Was she suddenly afraid that she was giving too much of herself away? She knew their relationship was going to end once her business was up and running, so was it beginning to occur to her that she was falling in love with him all over again, and it would break her heart to do so?

He smiled grimly. Simone had spectacularly fallen in with his plan. What he hadn't expected was that he too might find it hard to let her go at the end of the day. Without a doubt he would miss her in his bed. He had never found a woman who aroused him so deeply, who helped him find depths within himself that he never knew existed. But there was more to Simone than just sex, and Cade was beginning to realise that walking away might not be as easy as he'd first imagined.

The sun hadn't even reached its first tentative fingers above the horizon when he set off, but there was enough light to see by, and every fifteen minutes he checked on Simone, relieved to find her skin cool now and her breathing steady. As soon as they reached Airlie Beach he carried her ashore to the waiting car he'd ordered, and despite Simone's protests insisted on taking her straight to the hospital.

'I don't need a hospital or even a doctor,' she insisted, even though she was still in a great deal of pain. 'You're worrying too much.'

'Better safe than sorry,' Cade declared, and Simone thought that he sounded like her mother. He'd certainly been behaving like a mother hen. The thing was she didn't want him to feel sorry for her. She wanted him by her side for the rest of her life, and if she couldn't have that then she didn't want him near her at all.

She ought to have known from the very beginning that such an arrangement would never work, that she would end up getting hurt. It had been pathetic of her to agree to Cade's conditions. Except that their relationship had been overwhelmingly exciting. She couldn't deny that. Virtually every second spent in his company had been like living the dream—and now the dream had come to an end. She had woken to reality, to the fact that although she was still in love with him she would never mean anything to Cade.

Simone's ankle was x-rayed, and fortunately there was no ligament damage. 'It's just a sprain,' advised the doctor. 'Though very often they're more painful than torn ligaments. Keep your weight off it for a week or two and you'll be as right as rain.' He wasn't concerned about the bump on her head since she'd had no ill-effects from it.

A week or two! Which meant she couldn't leave, which

meant she'd have Cade fussing around her. And she didn't want that. It wouldn't be fair on him, for one thing, and for another she wasn't sure that she could cope mentally. He did her no good at all. No wonder the doctor on the island had declared her temperature a little high. It was Cade's fault, not her injury. She had seen the way some of the nurses looked at him, and suspected that their temperatures had risen too.

She was given a pair of crutches to help her get around, though she was warned to rest as much as possible, and when they got back to the beach house Cade insisted on making her comfortable on a sun-lounger on the deck. 'You can stay there the whole day long,' he declared. 'I'm your obedient servant.'

Simone raised an eyebrow. 'Is that so?'

'You don't want me looking after you?'

'Of course I do,' she said at once. She was actually not feeling too good, and guessed it was delayed reaction from the fall, though she didn't want to tell Cade this. 'Can you get me a glass of water, please?'

'Are you sure that's all you want?' The twinkle in his eyes suggested that he had other things in mind.

'I'm positive,' she announced.

And with that he had to be satisfied.

'Hi, Ros.'

Simone had been tempted to ignore her mobile phone, but Ros had been ringing for days now and she at least owed her friend some sort of explanation.

'At last!' exclaimed Ros. 'Why've you not been returning my calls?'

'I've hurt my ankle.'

There was raucous laughter at the other end. 'And that

stops you picking up your phone? Jeez, Simone, if I didn't know you better I'd say that you and Cade had got back together and were otherwise engaged.'

Simone drew in a swift breath and remained silent. She hadn't expected her friend to pick up on the truth so quickly.

'So you have! Crikey, Simone, what's got into you? The last time we spoke you said you thought he was after your business. Don't tell me he's got round you.' When Simone still said nothing, Ros continued, 'Where are you? I'm coming over. You and I need to talk.'

Because Cade wasn't at home, and because she needed someone to talk to, Simone gave her the address.

In half an hour Ros was there. 'Wow! This is Cade's place? Where's he got his millions from?' Her green eyes were huge as she looked around her.

'It's rented,' Simone informed her.

'It still must cost a fortune,' stated Ros explosively. 'I want to know what's going on between you two. But, first of all, what have you done to your ankle?' Her eyes had nearly popped when she saw the size of it.

'I slipped and sprained it, it's nothing,' declared Simone airily, balancing on her crutches. 'Let's go and sit down.'

'Not until I've seen over this incredible house. You stay there, I'll take a peek myself.' And before Simone could stop her, Ros was off on a whirlwind tour.

'Only one bedroom in use, I see,' she said with a knowledgeable smile when she joined Simone out on the deck.

Simone grimaced. 'I couldn't help myself.' Not for anything was she going to tell her friend that sleeping with Cade was a condition of their deal.

'So the old devil's got you back in his bed, has he? Are you still afraid he's going to take the business off you?'

Simone winced, a sheepish expression in her eyes. 'I've realised I had no valid reason to distrust him.'

Ros grinned. 'Is that after he got you into his bed?'

'Trust you to think that,' shot back Simone.

'But the old magic's still there? You couldn't help yourself?' Ros lifted her thick black hair from the nape of her neck and stretched her body luxuriously. 'He always was a gorgeous devil.' And it looked as though she was having impure thoughts about him herself.

The sound of a car pulling on to the driveway stemmed Ros's next words.

'That's him,' announced Simone, and Ros rose from her seat as Cade approached.

A pair of dark trousers and a dark polo-shirt emphasised his raw sex appeal, and Simone could guess at the emotions careering through her friend's body. Ros had always fancied Cade, and why wouldn't she? He had to be the sexiest man around.

'Ros Fletcher! Long time no see. You've certainly grown up.' Cade took in the full length of her tanned legs in her very brief shorts, her long, slender body and her hard, tight breasts thrusting against a low-cut top, finally meeting enquiring green eyes.

Simone felt jealousy shoot through her as she watched his appraisal. He didn't hide the fact that he liked what he saw. And Ros, given a chance, would play him for all he was worth.

Then his eyes switched to Simone and they softened. 'Are you OK?'

Warmth flooded through her. She smiled and nodded, not trusting herself to speak.

'So how did you find us?' he asked Ros.

'I phoned my friend and she said she was lonely. Actually, she didn't say that, but it's been so long since we got together that I sort of insisted.'

Cade smiled. 'Well, I'm glad Simone's had company. I didn't like to leave her in her present condition, but business called. Are you staying for lunch?'

Ros shook her head. 'People to see, things to do. But thanks for the offer. I'll see you again soon, Simone. Bye for now.' And with a swift kiss—for both of them—she was gone.

'Did she really invite herself?' asked Cade, sitting down on the edge of Simone's sun-lounger and taking one of her hands into his.

Simone nodded. 'But I wanted her here. We're good friends, I miss her.' She pulled her hands away. She'd seen the warning signals and now must be careful.

'Did you tell her about us?'

'About you forcing me to be your mistress?'

The word 'mistress' had Cade hardening his eyes. 'If that's how you still see it.'

'Is there any other way?' she returned. 'It's the truth. But I didn't tell her, no, so you're quite safe. Your character's still intact.'

Cade drew in a sharp breath but held on to his temper. 'What excuse did you give for us living together?'

'I didn't need to give her one.'

'She thought we'd resumed our relationship?'

Simone nodded.

'That's good.' He heaved himself up. 'I'll go and see about lunch.'

Simone found herself trembling when he'd gone. It was hard, trying to distance herself from him when he could demolish her defences with one glance out of his gorgeous golden eyes. But she had to be strong, because otherwise she'd give her all and then be thrown into a pit of despair when he'd finished with her. She wanted to end their relationship with her head held high, not be beaten down and made to feel worthless.

In the kitchen Cade took out ham and tomatoes, and fresh bread that had been delivered earlier, but all the time he was thinking about Simone. He couldn't help wondering whether she'd actually confided in her friend. She'd always been close to Ros, they told each other everything.

Perhaps Simone had been the one to make the phone call. Perhaps Ros knew about their situation, and that was why she'd hurried away when he'd arrived, because if she hadn't she'd have told him exactly what she thought of him.

He watched Simone closely as they ate their lunch, and was forced to admit that she didn't look guilty of anything. She was pale, very pale, which he guessed was due to the pain, but otherwise she seemed very relaxed.

'How's your ankle holding up?' Heavens, he didn't want to be talking about her injury, he didn't even want to talk. Despite everything, he wanted to press that excitingly sexy body against his; he wanted to kiss and touch and have her screaming for mercy.

He hated himself for wanting her while she was incapacitated, especially as she seemed to have cooled towards him, and yet there was nothing he could do about it. His body had a mind of its own where Simone was concerned.

Simone saw the fleet of changing expressions on Cade's face and wondered what he was thinking. He'd never been an open book, she'd never been able to read him, but there was something different about him today. 'Are you having problems with the business?' she asked.

Cade shook his head. 'Everything's going according to plan, I'm glad to say. What made you think that?'

'Nothing. Well, actually, you seem preoccupied.'

'The machinations of a business mind,' he informed her with a smile designed to set her mind at rest. 'Sometimes it's hard to switch off.'

Except when he was making fantastic love, thought Simone. He was well and truly switched off then. Or switched on, whichever way you liked to look at it. But she still felt that he had something on his mind.

She soon found out—and actually she was relieved.

'I think it would be better if you slept in one of the other rooms,' Cade announced later that evening. 'I'm concerned that I might hurt your ankle in my sleep. You're being incredibly brave, but I know it must be painful.'

'It does hurt, yes,' agreed Simone, even though she felt certain that his excuse was a feeble one. And this change in Cade worried her. Was he covering something up? Was everything not going according to plan, despite him saying otherwise? And, if this was the case, had he any intention of telling her? She'd give him a day or two, and then—

'Let's go and sort you out,' he said, cutting into her thoughts.

Simone was thankful there weren't any stairs, or he'd have had to carry her, and that would have been fatal. It would have been impossible for them to come into close contact and not end up making love. It was a given.

Perhaps he really was feeling sorry for her. Perhaps that was all there was to it. He'd decided he'd punished her enough. Either that or he thought her ankle was punishment. She'd paid her dues. He had no use for her any more.

Simone felt saddened at the thought. Not to have Cade kiss her ever again. Not to feel his hands touching and inciting, abrading her skin in a way unique to him, setting her lips alight, setting her whole body on fire, making love to her in spectacular Cade fashion.

Another thought struck her—unless he was doing it because of the way she'd run from him when she'd hurt her ankle, when she'd told him in no uncertain terms that she wanted to go home. He was literally taking her at her word and finishing their agreement—could that be it?

Once her ankle was better would it be the end of any intimacy? Which prompted her to wonder whether he would also walk away from the business side of their arrangement. Would she be left to finish what he had started? Would he, in fact, withdraw his funding?

'I'll take this one,' she said, and although she had fleetingly thought she might choose the room furthest away she selected the one next to him instead.

Imprudent or what?

The bed was already made up, and Cade fetched her clothes from his wardrobe and hung them in hers. Even her underwear he transferred. They looked ridiculously small and delicate in his hands—and very personal! She wondered if he had any idea how she felt about him handling them. Or even whether he experienced *any* emotions. She would love to get inside his mind.

'I'll leave you, then,' he said gruffly.

Simone nodded.

'You'll be all right?'

'Yes.' Actually she would never be right again. Didn't Cade realise he was crucifying her, that she might die in the night of a broken heart? Besides, she needed his help in the shower, but if he couldn't think that far ahead then she wasn't going to ask.

He kissed her briefly on the forehead—the sort of kiss one would give a child—and the door closed behind him. Simone wanted to kick it. She would have done if she'd had two good legs.

Damn Cade!

She didn't want him to leave her alone. She wanted his body, hot and strong, feverish and exciting. She wanted him to take her mind off the pain that throbbed through her ankle and threatened to give her a sleepless night. Off the general feeling of something being not quite right with her body. It was nothing she could put her finger on, and was probably the after-effects of the fall, but if anyone could make her forget it then Cade could.

Leaning her crutches against the wall beside the shower, she dragged off her clothes and stepped into the cubicle. It was more confined than the one in the other room, and putting all her weight on one leg didn't leave much room to manoeuvre. But somehow she managed, turning on the tap and standing beneath its welcoming spray as she lathered her body.

What she hadn't counted on was the floor becoming slippy from the bubbles. On two legs it wouldn't have mattered, but on one she lost her balance and found herself sliding down the shower wall, ending in a heap in the basin.

She must have cried out, though she wasn't aware of it, because Cade came running.

In seconds she was heaved to her feet and carried across to the bed, where he laid her down with incredible tenderness. 'What was I thinking, leaving you like that?' he asked forcefully. 'Now you've hurt yourself all over again. Damn, I'm an idiot.'

'It wasn't your fault,' said Simone, while beneath her breath she hoped he'd had a change of heart and would take her back into his bed.

'Yes, it was, I've made matters worse by trying to be heroic. Damn it, Simone, I should never have insisted you sleep alone. The bed's big enough, for goodness' sake, for us to share and not even touch.'

'Is that possible?' she asked. 'considering the electricity that sparks between us?' Where had those words popped from? He'd just made it clear he didn't want to sleep with her and yet she'd baited him.

'Hell, it isn't,' he agreed. 'I wasn't looking forward to being alone tonight.'

'Neither was I,' she said quietly, hiding none of the hunger that raged through her.

He groaned then, and, lifting her into his arms, he carried her back into the master bedroom, kicking the door shut behind him.

CHAPTER ELEVEN

'I'M SORRY, Cade, I can't. My mother's more important.'

'Have you ever been to England?' Cade's eyes were cruelly dark, his whole body stiff with displeasure, as if he could hardly believe she had turned him down.

'No, but—'

'Then I insist. Treat it as a holiday, if you like. I bet you haven't had one of those in a long time.'

Since living with Cade it had been all holiday, thought Simone. She'd never done so little in the whole of her life. 'I don't need a holiday,' she declared, her violet eyes warring with his. 'And I haven't seen my mother since I hurt my ankle.'

'You speak to her every day.'

'That's different. She's not very well, actually. I'm staying, Cade, whether you like it or not. My mother's my first priority.'

The last two weeks had been sensationally explosive. Not the warring kind, the getting-it-together-in-bed kind. Ever heedful of her injury, Cade had introduced new and awesome ways of making love, his seduction techniques uniquely Cade, blowing her mind with alarming frequency.

But now they were on opposite sides of the fence. He was almost bristling with anger, and she couldn't understand why. It wasn't as if he owned her. Or did he think that he did? Did he still think that because he was helping her out he could dictate her every move?

In her mind she'd already paid her dues, over and over again. Even if it was in a very atypical way. And she was prepared to stand her ground. If his visit to England was so important, then he could go on his own. Some management crisis, he'd said, so he wouldn't want her hanging around. She'd be left on her own for most of the time. She'd much rather spend it with her mother. Poor darling, she'd so missed her visits.

'Besides,' Simone argued, 'if there should be any hitches with the redevelopment of the company then someone needs to be here.'

'There will be no problems,' he affirmed coldly.

Simone didn't see how he could be so sure. No matter how well plans were laid, something inevitably went wrong. 'Whatever,' she responded with a shrug. 'But I'm staying, whether you like it or not. And if you don't want me to carry on living here then I'll go home.'

'You'll stay here,' he commanded, and Simone had never heard his voice so angry. Except perhaps when he had accused her all those years ago. A shiver ran down her spine. Cade had to learn that she didn't run to do his bidding every time he snapped his fingers. Becoming his mistress had been a pleasure, it was like living a dream, but as for anything else— Well, he could take a running jump. Discovering that she was in love with him, when all he felt was raw need and a desire to punish, was persecution enough.

She shrugged, knowing in her own mind that she'd rather be here than with her drunken father. 'When do you leave?'

'Shortly. What will you do with yourself, apart from visit your mother?'

'Check up on my assets,' she flared.

Simone was beautiful in her anger, acknowledged Cade. Did she know that she aroused him simply by glaring? Did she know that his testosterone levels were rising so rapidly that he was prepared to risk missing his plane to make love to her one last time?

'*Your* assets?' he queried, deliberately hardening his voice. It was the only way he knew to stamp on these feelings that persisted in making themselves felt. 'I didn't realise you had any.'

It had been wrong not to involve her in the upgrade of the charter company, but he'd wanted everything to be a pleasant surprise. He hadn't thought that in the beginning, of course. He'd simply seen it as a further form of punishment. Now, though, he wanted to present her with something extraordinary. He wanted to see her expression when the whole new face of MM Charters was revealed.

Simone winced. Did he have to make it quite so clear that she was penniless and relied on him heavily? 'Have a good trip,' she said tightly, and turned and walked away.

Nevertheless it was all she could do not to call him back and fling herself into his arms. She wanted to confess that she would miss him, but she dared not. It would tell him that she'd grown to love him again; it would give him even more ammunition to throw in her face.

Instead she headed for the ocean, slipping out of her sandals and curling her toes in the soft white sand. It was strange. She had lived here all her life, and yet had never really appreciated what was right in front of her. People would pay the earth to have this right on their doorstep. She edged nearer to the ocean and let the clear water wash over her toes. It was warm and sensual, and she wanted to share it with Cade.

Instead he was leaving her. Was it too late, she wondered, to change her mind, go with him to England, share his life there? To see what he had made of himself. One half of her wanted to go, the other knew that her mother needed her more. It was not only that she wanted to see her mother, she desired time to herself. She needed to assess her feelings and she couldn't do that while Cade was around.

When she returned to the house he had gone. And instead of feeling relieved Simone felt sad. Sad and lonely. She didn't even know how long he'd be away. But there was another reason she wanted to stay: there was something she seriously needed to talk over with her mother.

At the nursing home later Simone was shocked at the difference in her parent. She knew that Pamela had picked up a bug, but she looked terrible. She lay in her bed with no colour at all in her cheeks, though she smiled bravely when Simone approached.

'My darling daughter, how's your ankle?'

'It's better—well, almost,' admitted Simone. 'How about you? I know you said you weren't feeling too good, but you look far worse than I imagined.'

Pamela Maxwell pulled a wry face. 'It's something going round. It's laid us all low. I'll be as right as rain in a few days.'

It looked more than that to Simone, but she let it pass. She'd ask a member of staff later what was going on.

'Sit down,' invited her mother. 'How's Cade? I expected him to come with you.'

Simone dropped into an easy chair beside the bed. 'He's on his way to England right at this very minute. Some crisis needs his attention.'

Pamela frowned. 'Why didn't you go with him?'

'And leave you?' returned Simone sharply. 'Not likely.'

Her mother looked at her, a thoughtful expression in her eyes. 'So I was the excuse, was I?'

Simone smiled weakly. 'You know me too well.'

'How are you getting on with him?'

'I think I'm falling in love again,' she confessed, before she'd even had time to wonder whether this was the right thing to be telling her parent.

'Is that a bad thing?' asked her mother, not looking in the least surprised.

'It is when he's still intent on punishing me,' answered Simone.

'Punishing?' Pamela frowned.

Simone realised then that she hadn't told her about their deal. Her mother didn't know that she was paying with her body. 'Oh, you know, he wants his pound of flesh. He has me at his beck and call all day long, intent on humiliating me, because of the money I supposedly lost him.'

'You should let me talk to him,' said Pamela indignantly, some of the colour coming back into her cheeks. 'He can't do this to you. The past is the past. He's made his mark now. I never realised he was a man to hold a grudge.'

'There's more,' confessed Simone, closing her eyes and speaking in no more than a breathy whisper; she had to get this out quickly before she lost her nerve. 'I think I might be pregnant with his baby.'

At first she'd put her missed period down to the upheaval in her life, and then her queasiness down to her fall. But it had gradually become clear that there was a far more serious reason.

'I didn't realise you had that sort of relationship with Cade.' Pamela Maxwell's face held no condemnation, simply concern for her beloved daughter.

Simone clamped her lips and nodded. 'I couldn't help

myself.' She didn't want to say that he'd forced her. And she knew that if she *was* pregnant it had happened the first time Cade had ever made love to her, because he'd taken precautions ever since.

'Have you told him?'

'I can't, I daren't,' whispered Simone, every ounce of colour draining from her face.

'He has every right to know.'

Simone knew her mother was making sense, but how could she tell him, given their circumstances? He might even think that she had got pregnant deliberately; she certainly hadn't hidden any of her feelings. 'He'll hate me for it,' she said, her voice little more than a croak now. 'I can't tell him, not yet at least. Not until I'm sure.' Perhaps not even then. Her mother didn't know the half of it.

'Don't leave it too long,' said Pamela softly. 'It won't be fair on him.'

Fair, thought Simone. Fairness wasn't a part of Cade's vocabulary. What Cade wanted, Cade took.

'Do you want this baby?' asked her mother gently.

'No! Yes! Of course I do.'

'And how will Cade feel, do you think? What sort of a relationship do you have? Will he marry you?'

'Mother, people don't get married these days because they're expecting a baby.'

Pamela Maxwell pursed her lips. 'I thought I'd brought you up differently to that. Do you love Cade?'

Simone nodded.

'But he doesn't return your love? He still thinks you've let him down?'

'Yes.'

'Then it's up to you to change his mind. And sooner rather

than later. He needs to know, Simone. And you need to know conclusively as well. Go and see Dr Hanson.'

Simone nodded again.

Sleep proved elusive that night. If she really was pregnant—and she couldn't dispute the fact that the signs were there—then she had a real problem. If she told Cade he would be angrier than she had ever seen him, and if she didn't tell him and he subsequently found out there would still be hell to pay. She was in a no-win situation, and she couldn't see any way out of it.

The next morning she ventured into Cade's study again and sat down at his desk. Splaying her hands on the glass top, she looked about her. Through the window was a view of the inner courtyard and the pool, and Simone couldn't help wondering whether he had ever sat here and watched her swimming. Had he lusted after her body, congratulating himself on his devious plot? Had everything been planned down to the finest detail here in this room?

Except that he couldn't have imagined that it would end this way.

Nor could she, if the truth were known.

As she sat there thinking about him, about the way he set her body alight, about the way she had too-willingly agreed to his plan—something she wished now with all her heart that she had never consented to—the phone rang, startling her, making her feel guilty for being here.

She felt even guiltier when she heard Cade's voice.

'Where are you?' she asked, feeling her heartrate increase, unconsciously putting a hand to her stomach, painfully aware of the possibility of a new life growing inside her. Born of their hunger for each other's bodies. She winced at this thought. A baby should be created by love, not because of shameless desire.

'I'm at Heathrow. How are you? Did you sleep well?'

'Not really.'

'You missed me?'

Simone was silent so long that he spoke again. 'Is something wrong?'

'No! Why should there be?' she asked quickly.

'You sound—different. How's your mother?'

Simone grasped the excuse.

'Not well.'

'I'm sorry.'

I bet you are, she thought, relieved that the attention had been taken away from herself. She had a lot of thinking to do before she told Cade about her baby—*their* baby. He'd be so angry, he'd blame her. And he'd insist on marrying her for the child's sake, which was the last thing she wanted. Yes, she loved Cade, but he didn't love her. He'd never love her again, not the way he had. She'd be better off out of his life.

'What are your plans now?' she asked, realising the seconds were ticking away and he'd expect some response. 'Are you going straight to your office, or home to sleep? What time is it there?'

'It's eight in the evening and, yes, I'm going home.' His voice dropped an octave lower. 'I wish you were with me. I'll miss you in my bed.'

Of course he would! He'd miss her to feed his fantasies. It was all she was good for. If he had any idea... No, she mustn't let her thoughts wander in that direction. It really didn't bear thinking about.

'Did you miss *me* last night?' he asked when she remained silent.

'Yes,' came her faint response, because of course she'd missed him. They hadn't spent a night apart since she'd become his mistress. The bed had felt cold and empty, and her deeply troubled thoughts had kept her awake

His voice dropped an octave. 'I'll try not to be any longer than necessary. Be good, and give my regards to your mother.' With that the phone went dead.

Sitting at his desk, waiting for her heartbeats to subside, she tried to imagine what it would be like to tell Cade that he was going to become a father, wondering if she would ever find the courage to do so. She opened a folder with MM Charters written in neat black writing on the outside.

The file was very thick by now, and by the time she'd finished scanning the contents Simone was completely over-whelmed by how much Cade had spent, and had still to spend. Her jaw went slack as the figures revealed themselves. They were far higher than anything she'd envisaged. Triple the cost since the last time she'd looked.

Whether she liked it or not, Cade Dupont *was* the new company. He owned it totally. She could not see how, not in a million years, he would let her get away with running it herself. He would never, ever distance himself from it. He couldn't. It would be foolhardy. It was *his* investment, he'd want to keep his eye on it.

She'd sold her soul to him—for what? Nada, niente, zilch.

And the fact that she was pregnant compounded the issue. How could she run a company when she had a child to look after? No, she had lost and Cade had won. Even if it hadn't been his intention in the beginning, it had worked out that way.

It saddened her to think that the company her parents had set up was now falling into the hands of Cade Dupont. Cade Dupont successful businessman. With an eye for a good deal. *Also*, whispered a voice inside her head, *Cade Dupont, your baby's father!*

Simone drew in deep breaths of air, expelling them noisily. Pressing her hands down on the desk, she pushed herself up. One half of her wanted to run—she didn't want him to find out about his child—the other half knew that she had to stay and face him regardless of the consequences.

She stripped off her clothes and dived into the pool naked, swimming length after length after length until she was too tired to swim any more.

Another night was spent tossing and turning and having nightmares about Cade.

She kept expecting him to ring again, was disappointed when he didn't, even though she told herself that she didn't care. *She didn't!* The longer he was away, the longer she could put off deciding whether to tell him about the baby.

It was ironic that she should become pregnant now, when she'd so desperately wanted a baby when married to Gerard. It was something they ought to have discussed before they'd got married, but they hadn't. Maybe her nagging him to start a family was what had sent him into the arms of another woman.

Not that she really cared at this stage. Meeting Gerard again had made her realise what a lucky escape she'd had. He definitely wasn't the man for her. Cade was. But Cade didn't want her. His reasons for bedding her were mercenary.

Hell, what a mess she was in.

CHAPTER TWELVE

SIMONE didn't know whether to feel relief or fear when Cade returned five days later. He hadn't phoned again, except to say when he was due—and that had been a short conversation because he'd been about to board his plane. Simone had heard her own jerky voice in response to his, and had known that she'd been in grave danger of giving away the turmoil that was confusing her brain and causing her limbs to shake like the leaves on a tree in a strong wind.

Her heart began to panic the second she heard the car pull up, and she watched from a window as Cade got out. She had almost forgotten how handsome, how imposing he was. How that tall, lithe figure clad in a light-grey suit, which hid none of the breadth of his shoulders or the powerful muscles in his long legs, could spin her senses into disarray—made worse by the certain knowledge that she was carrying his child.

Simone had paid a visit to her doctor, who had confirmed her pregnancy, and she had returned to the beach house and cried and cried until there were no tears left. In one way it had been a relief that Cade wasn't there, because there would have been no way she would have been able to hide her upset from him. She still wasn't sure whether to tell him. One day he would have to know, it would be unfair of her not to confess. But now, after his long flight and all the troubles he'd had to deal with in England, probably wasn't the right time— if there ever would be one!

She'd thought about it a lot, in fact she'd thought about nothing else, and all she could envisage was Cade's anger. Again she had a feeling he'd blame her, that he might even say she'd got pregnant deliberately. He couldn't have failed to notice that she'd fallen back in love with him, and having his baby would ensure that he stayed in her life.

So many scenarios had raced through her mind that she'd become dizzy by it all. Now, watching him, seeing that hard, tanned face, feeling the tightening of her muscles, the way her heart began to race, she felt even more confused.

Cade's intense eyes scanned the building as he approached, and Simone stepped back. If theirs had been a real relationship she would have run out to greet him. They would have stood out there in the hot sunshine, and he'd have grabbed her and kissed her and they would have shown each other in every way possible how much they had been missed.

As things stood she was more than a little apprehensive. What if she gave herself away? What if he guessed there was something wrong and kept hounding her to tell him? How would she handle it?

Her heart pounded so fiercely that it hurt. She risked another look out of the window. He stood tall and proud, his head held perhaps even more arrogantly than usual, and she couldn't help wondering whether he'd taken the opportunity while he was on the other side of the world to assess their situation.

It made her realise that she really knew very little about the way Cade's mind worked these days. In the past, in those heady, halcyon days when they'd been truly in love, she had known everything about him. But he'd returned a total stranger, a hard businessman with an eye for increasing his already more-than-successful charter business.

It was hard, in fact it was impossible, to believe that he was helping her out of the kindness of his heart. He'd used her, he'd taken her business failure as an excuse and forced her to sell her body to him. And now she was pregnant with his child.

Nevertheless her mind became suddenly clear. This baby was hers. Hers alone. She wouldn't tell Cade; he didn't deserve to be told. He had used and abused her— Well, perhaps not abused—she had been a willing partner—but his method of persuasion left a lot to be desired.

She'd been weak, too weak, letting her heart rule her head. Now she had to suffer the consequences for the rest of her life. No, she wouldn't tell him.

He had reached the house. She heard the door open and turned slowly, waiting, trying to ignore the hammer beats of her heart. She waited in vain. Cade went straight to his room. The room they had once shared. The room she had moved out of immediately he'd left for England.

Once she'd discovered that she was pregnant, it had felt wrong to be lying in his bed.

Contrarily, disappointment filled her, deep, dark disappointment. What she'd been hoping for she didn't know, but she hadn't expected to be ignored.

She charged into the room after him. 'Aren't you going to say hello?' There was a proud lift to her chin, her eyes burned a challenging, brilliant amethyst, and she dared him to ignore it.

He looked at her with those sensual, golden eyes of his, eyes that threatened to destroy every ounce of the self-composure she'd struggled with. 'I was simply disposing of my case. How are you, Simone? Have you missed me? No, don't answer that; it's clear you have or you wouldn't have come charging in here like an enraged bull.' He held out his arms, and Simone felt an unwelcome urge to fling herself into them.

Cade had wondered what sort of a reception he would get from Simone. To his astonishment he had missed her like hell, and had wanted to ring her often, except that both commitments and the time difference between the two countries had made it near impossible.

He wished that she'd agreed to accompany him. He had wanted to show off his success in England and Europe. He'd wanted her to enjoy it, see for herself what her own company would be like when it began running again. And when she wouldn't go he'd interpreted it as rejection. He wasn't used to handling rejection. Even when he'd phoned her from Heathrow he'd been able to tell from her voice that she didn't want to talk to him.

He should have been glad, he supposed, it would make their inevitable parting all the easier to bear. But he hadn't been able to get her out of his mind. Now she was here in the flesh before him, all fire and brimstone, demanding to know why he hadn't immediately sought her out.

He had never seen her look more beautiful. Her auburn hair, loose from its normal constricting band, flamed around her face, and her unusual eyes were filled with fury. Her soft, pink parted lips tormented his senses, made him want to pull her against him and kiss her until she begged for mercy.

Did it mean that she had missed him in bed beside her? Because he sure as hell had missed her. Never had his apartment felt so empty—even though she'd never been there. She'd got beneath his skin like a disease, and there had been times when he'd wished with all his heart that he'd never returned to Australia.

But he had, and he'd made her his mistress, and although his

thoughts had been to ditch her at the end of it all he was beginning to wonder whether he'd have the strength of will to do so.

Even now, this very second, when she stood before him
with all the fires of hell burning in her breast, he wanted her.
Her hesitation seemed to take for ever. He was on the point
of turning away and pretending he didn't care when she
walked slowly into his arms.

She didn't throw herself at him; it was such a steady
process that he felt her reluctance and wondered at it.
Whatever was said about absence making the heart grow
fonder, it wasn't so in this case.

Nevertheless he folded his arms around her, feeling the
sweet softness of her against him, inhaling the heady fra-
grance that was spectacularly Simone's. He didn't kiss her,
even though he wanted to, he simply held her. And gradually
she relaxed, she lifted her chin and looked up at him.

He smiled. 'What's the matter, Simone? What's happened
to you while I've been gone?'

She felt a dangerous heat sweep through her body, but re-
maining calm became a priority. Cade had probably expected
her to welcome him with open arms, to declare that she had
missed him like hell. And when she hadn't he'd decided something was wrong.

So she needed to give him something to latch on to. 'Why
haven't you phoned me?' she questioned, flashing her eyes at
him, disregarding the heat consuming her, the need to be kissed,
to be made-love to as only Cade knew how. It was difficult,
ignoring it, but somehow she did, she hid the fire in her belly
and the hunger in her heart, and she looked at him hostilely.

'Apart from telling me when you'd arrived, and then again
to say you were coming back, you were remarkably silent.
Don't tell me that you were so busy you couldn't find a

moment to phone and see how I was? Out of sight out of mind, was that it?'

'You *did* miss me!'

There was such delight in his voice, such appreciation in his beautiful eyes, that Simone felt she'd gone too far. But as she didn't want him questioning her excessively she nodded instead. 'How could I not?' And she smiled.

When Cade smiled in response, when his arms tightened around her and he lowered his head to drop a kiss on her brow, she felt a whole army of sensations march through her body. If she closed her eyes she could imagine that nothing was wrong. She could pretend that Cade hadn't been away, that she wasn't facing the biggest challenge of her life.

Without even realising what she was doing, Simone dropped her head back, arching her neck, feeling a deep aching hunger inside her. It was her undoing. Cade took it as an invitation, and his mouth descended on hers in a kiss that threatened to sweep away her fears.

She was in very grave danger of allowing him back into her life, and some of her fear must have woven its way into her kiss because Cade withdrew and gave her a long, considering look through narrowed eyes. She tried to hold his gaze, but was afraid he'd read her secret, and so lowered her lids.

Cade dropped his arms and stepped back a pace. 'Time for this later,' he said gruffly. 'I need a shower and a change of clothes.'

Simone thought she heard a hard edge to his voice. Of course she could be mistaken, it could all be in her mind, but she didn't think so. She'd given away the fact that there was something wrong, and he wouldn't give in until he knew what it was. She would have to act like she'd never acted before if she wanted to keep her secret.

She was sitting outside when Cade reappeared, watching the sun sink slowly towards the horizon. Usually Simone enjoyed this time of day, but now she was as nervous as a kitten. And, damn it he not only looked gorgeous, in ivory linen trousers with a matching short-sleeved shirt, he smelled gorgeous too. Cedar, she thought, just a faint hint, enough to tantalise her senses, alert them to the fact that this man was an excitingly sexy male animal who had shared her bed and was the father of the child growing inside her.

She hated the way her thoughts always led back to the baby. Except how could she ignore it? Each morning now she felt unwell. She wasn't physically sick, but very close to it, and how she was going to hide this from Cade she didn't know.

He chose a chair opposite rather than next to her, and although Simone was grateful for the distance between them she found it even more disconcerting to have him facing her because she knew that his eyes would be on her all the time. There would be no escaping their scrutiny.

'So, what's been happening in my absence?' he asked. 'How's your mother?'

Simone knew very well that he didn't really want to be talking about her mother. She could see in his eyes that he had other things on his mind. But politeness seemed to be the name of the game—for the moment, anyway.

'She's getting better every day.'

'That's good. Next time you go, I'll come with you.'

'No!' Simone was shocked to hear the sharpness in her voice, but, goodness, she knew what her mother was like. She'd probably tell Cade about the baby, make it plain that he needed to share the responsibility.

It was a situation that didn't bear thinking about.

'No?' he queried, dark brows rising.

'She's not up to visitors yet,' she prevaricated. 'She doesn't mind me, but—'

'In other words you don't want me to go and see her?' asked Cade, an unnerving light in his eyes. 'You think I might upset her by bringing up the past?'

Simone clutched at the excuse. 'It's not something she's proud of, even though it was my father's doing. Or do you *still* think that I was involved?' She shot him a fiercely purple accusatory stare.

Cade stared back, and several long seconds passed when neither of them spoke, when she held her breath in anticipation. Finally, after an eternity of anguish on her part, he surprised her by saying, 'Actually, no.'

Simone raised her fine brows, scarcely able to believe what she had heard.

Cade continued, his golden eyes steady as he looked at her, and Simone fancied that she could see torment in their depths. 'The evidence was there all those years ago. I had no reason to accept your word, not when your father told me that you and he were in league with each other.'

'But I loved you, Cade. I would never have done anything like that to you. And if you'd truly loved me you'd have known it, you'd have realised my father was lying.' It proved that his love had never been as strong as hers. If indeed he'd ever loved her.

She'd like to bet that his heart had never felt empty, broken, as though life held no meaning any more. Hell, no! If he had, if he'd been as upset as she'd been, he'd have answered her phone calls.

Yes, he'd been stung by her father—but he'd hurt her more. What was money compared to love? True love lasted a lifetime. It transcended all evil. Cade had proven beyond any shadow of doubt that he'd never loved her. Nor did he love her now. They had great sex together, but if she had hopes of anything else then she was a bigger fool than she'd imagined.

'It's supposed to make me feel better, is it?' she asked scathingly. 'You confessing that you now believe I had no part to play in my father's dastardly plot? Well, let me tell you something—'

'No, let me tell you,' he cut in fiercely, his eyes blazing into hers. 'Your father was very convincing. I didn't want to believe him, but I had no choice. And I was afraid that if I stayed and tackled you about it you'd feed me a pack of lies and I'd believe them—and probably regret it for ever. As far as I was concerned, a clean break was the best thing. If I've wronged you, I'm sorry, Simone. But, if anyone's to blame, it's your father.'

Deep down inside Simone knew this, but too many years had passed for her to forgive and forget. Cade had destroyed her faith in human nature; he had almost destroyed her life. She'd thought that marrying Gerard would make her forget about him, but even that had been a fool's dream.

She sighed. What she wouldn't give for a simple life.

While they were clearing the air it would have been a good time to tell him about the baby, but she couldn't do it. All it would do was throw a further spanner into the works. Cade's admission that he was wrong in doubting her had been given reluctantly, and if she told him now that he was about to become a father all hell would break loose.

He'd most certainly want her to commit to him for ever, and how could she do that when she knew he didn't love her?

'I don't think my father can shoulder all the blame here, Cade,' she finally said sadly. 'You could have stayed here and we could have sorted the whole sorry mess out. I could have tried harder to explain, but it's all in the past now. Forgive me, Cade, but I've no wish to carry on this conversation. I'm going to bed.'

'At this hour?' he asked, glancing at his watch. 'I've been away for almost a week, I've worked all the hours God made, and now I want to spend time with you. Not arguing, not glaring at each other like two caged animals. I want a civilised conversation.'

'Or maybe it's something more you're after?' she riposted. 'Like me in your bed?'

Cade began to smile. 'Now you're talking. I've not been able to think about anything else on the flight over. I've missed you, Simone. More than I expected.'

'And that's supposed to make me feel good, is it?' She sat that little bit straighter, fixing her violet eyes on his. 'Is it all I'm good for? I've had time to think about my situation,' she added crisply. 'I think I've paid my dues, over and over again. I want out, Cade. I want out now.'

'Is that so?' Dark brows lifted, his gorgeous eyes boring into hers. She'd been about to get to her feet, but his gaze pinned her. 'We have a contract, you and I,' he reminded her tersely. 'And I expect you to honour it.'

He pulled her close to his body, making Simone insanely aware that even though he was angry his state of arousal was unparalleled.

She wasn't doing too badly in the erotic stakes herself. Everything felt more intense; she wanted to pull his head down to hers, she wanted him to make love to her here, now. It would be fierce and furious and utterly mind-blowing. She wanted him...

She slammed her thoughts back to where they had come from. Letting Cade make love to her would lock her back into being his mistress. She'd never escape. So she stiffened her body, ignoring the serious sensations that were turning her blood to fire, and pushed against him.

Immediately Cade let her go. His face became a picture of disbelief and fury as he stepped back a pace. 'I want to know what the hell's going on,' he fumed. 'But not tonight. Go to your bed alone, if that's your wish—and don't think I haven't noticed that you're not sleeping in my room.'

Simone almost gave in then and almost flung herself back into his arms. It was hard being strong. She wanted him so much; her whole body ached for him, each limb filled with need, her heart sitting sadly in her breast because it was being thwarted. But she definitely needed space between her and Cade, time to think, to plan—to plan her whole life, in fact.

Of necessity she had to keep him at a distance, but the thought that he might never kiss her again, touch her skin, make her feel wondrously alive, made her weep inside. Shards of ice slithered down her spine, she could feel them taking over slow inch by slow inch. Soon she would become frozen in time.

She fled to her room and collapsed on the bed. Even though she knew it was for the best, it still crucified her. She curled up, her knees under her chin, her arms folded around herself, and it was like this that Cade found her several hours later. Fast asleep.

He stood looking down at her, and wondered what had happened in his absence to make Simone so fiercely against him. They couldn't go on in this manner, that was for sure. He either disappeared out of her life completely, or—

Simone's mobile phone rang, and when it became clear that she wasn't going to wake Cade answered it himself.

'Who's that?'

The voice was slurred and angry, and Cade knew instantly that it was Simone's father.

'It's Cade,' he answered, walking out of the room so as not to disturb her.

'What the hell are you doing with my daughter's phone?'

'She's asleep.'

'What's wrong with her?'

'Nothing.' But if this was the way Matthew Maxwell normally spoke to his daughter then Cade was glad that he'd answered. The man was a menace.

'So she's still living with you, is she?' grunted the older man. 'Needs her head examining, if you ask me.'

'I didn't ask,' retorted Cade. 'Would you like to leave a message?'

'Tell her to get round here.'

'Why?'

It seemed like a reasonable question to Cade, but Simone's father saw it differently. 'Why? You're daring to ask me why I want my daughter? She belongs here, that's why, she has a duty towards me.'

Cade saw a red mist rise in front of his eyes.

'Simone owes you nothing, Mr Maxwell. In fact, she ought to hate your guts. You fooled me into accepting that she was in league with you when you robbed me of my inheritance. All these years I believed it. I hurt her irreparably. I've finally come to my senses, but I think I can safely say that Simone has no wish to come back home.'

She might not want to spend time with him either—but that was another story. Matthew Maxwell didn't need to hear about that. 'I'll tell Simone you called when she wakes tomorrow.' He heard a hiss of displeasure from the other end and the phone went dead.

Cade slipped the phone back on to Simone's dresser, and stood there a moment looking at her. Her rich auburn hair fanned the pillow and accentuated the pale translucency of her skin. There were faint shadows beneath her eyes, and it was all he could do not to bow down and kiss her. He wanted her so badly it hurt.

He'd thought about her the whole time on his return flight. He'd imagined their impassioned love-making, absence making need grow stronger. He had never dreamt that she would turn against him.

It had been fatal, letting her stay behind. He should have insisted she accompany him, then she wouldn't have had the chance to distance herself. She must have done a lot of thinking while he was away, decided that she couldn't carry on with this arrangement any longer.

She'd certainly made it perfectly clear that she didn't love him. She enjoyed making love—in fact he'd never known a woman who abandoned herself so completely, who had such a voracious appetite—but what she'd been doing was making the best of a bad situation, all in the name of saving her company.

And now that he knew for sure she hadn't been instrumental in his downfall he felt guilty for pressurising her into becoming his mistress. She must have felt that she was selling her soul to the devil. It didn't sit well on his shoulders.

He pressed a light kiss to her brow, then left, showering and going to bed himself. But he was unable to sleep, rising early, swimming a few energetic lengths of the pool, and he was sitting out on the deck when Simone came to find him.

She was dressed in a red top and shorts, her hair tied severely back, and she looked as though she was set to make trouble. There were patches of high colour in her cheeks now, and her eyes were fiercely aggressive.

'Our situation's become untenable,' she said without

preamble. 'I think we should call an end to our partner-ship—if it can be called that. I appreciate all you've done for MM Charters, you've spent far more than I ever intended you to, so it's yours. I'll see my lawyer tomorrow and get the papers drawn up.'

CHAPTER THIRTEEN

CADE was stunned. So it was the amount of money he'd spent that had caused the difference in Simone. She'd been struggling with her conscience—despite paying for it in a way that had suited them both. There'd been times when he'd felt they were in a true relationship, when he'd actually forgotten that he was out for revenge.

It had usually happened when they were making love. He had never met a woman who fulfilled his needs so magnificently, who met him head-on, whose hunger equalled his in every direction. Simone by no means had given the impression that she was simply meeting the demands he'd made on her. She'd given herself freely and utterly.

In the beginning he'd exulted at her unbridled response; he'd seen her downfall being far more spectacular than he'd envisaged. Quite when the idea had no longer given him so much pleasure, he had no idea. It had crept up on him. He hadn't even known himself until now.

Until Simone's rejection.

Until she'd turned the tables!

His heartrate increased until it felt like the blow of a hammer striking metal, loud and strong, deeply painful, and he realised that he didn't want to let her go. To hell with the charter business, there were more important things in life. In fact he should be the one pandering to her—apologizing, even.

Except that it went against the grain. He'd done what he'd done in all good faith. He had truly believed she was at fault. It had taken her rejection to remove the blinkers from his eyes.

'And how would you know how much I've spent?' he asked, springing to his feet and facing her.

'Because I've looked through the papers in your office,' she snapped. 'You've poured in so much money that you knew at the end of the day I'd have no option but to hand the business over to you. You knew my conscience would make me do that. Oh, you were clever, yes, by saying that we'd be partners— but you knew very well what my reaction would be when I saw the final figures. So I'm not giving you that pleasure. It's yours, lock, stock and barrel.'

'You're embarrassed that I've spent so much?' Cade found her excuse weak in the extreme. Most girls would have snapped his hands off.

'Not embarrassed,' she retorted. 'In fact, I should have realised. But the figures I saw exceeded my wildest imagination. No man would do that, Cade, unless he had an ulterior motive. So it's yours. I'm moving back home.'

'The hell you are!' exclaimed Cade, unable to bear the thought of losing Simone. 'A deal's a deal. Until the business is up and running again, you're mine. Don't ever forget that.'

Simone shivered. Cade sounded as though he meant it. But how could he unless he held her against her will? And there was no chance of that. 'You're not my keeper,' she insisted hotly, her eyes flashing purple sparks. 'And since I'm giving you the company there's nothing you can do about it. Take it, it's yours. I'm going to pack.' And she swung on her heel.

But Cade was having none of it. His hand caught her

shoulder and spun her round to face him. His golden eyes were as fierce as hers. 'Is there any woman on the face of this earth who'd throw such a gift back in the face of her benefactor? You have to be seriously insane.'

'Perhaps I am. Perhaps I've had time to come to my senses. Have you no idea how demeaning my position is?' She continued to glare, standing firm in front of him even though she wished herself a million miles away. What would Cade say, she wondered, if he knew that a new life was forming inside her? A life that belonged to him as well.

He'd either run a mile or demand she marry him. There would be no in between. She guessed it would be the second option. But marriage to a man who for many years had believed her capable of duplicity did not give her pleasure. Cade was well versed in the art of getting what he wanted— she had found that out first-hand. So she had to stand firm, do what she felt was right for herself.

'I'm sorry you feel that way,' he replied. 'But I'm not budging an inch.'

Their eyes met, and held for several long seconds, and much to her disgust, Simone felt herself weakening. She mentally shook her head, brought her thoughts back into order. She had to do this, she had no other choice. 'I'm sorry too, Cade, but my mind's made up.' If she didn't get out now, she never would. He'd find out her secret and there would be no going back.

Cade was a man of honour. If he discovered he had fathered a child, then he would see it as his duty to provide and care for that child. And if it meant marrying her then he would do so—whether he loved her or not. He would see it as his duty.

Simone watched as his nostrils flared, and she saw his

fingers curl into fists at his side. 'I'm not a man to go back on my word, Simone. If you really abhor me that much, then once your company is up and running again I'll do the walking. I'll go back to England and you can forget me.'

For a few seconds Simone stared at him in stunned silence. What was he saying? He'd spent all this money, and yet he would walk away and just give it to her? How could he do that? Why? It didn't make sense. 'You're an idiot,' she declared. 'You came over here with the intention of setting up business, and now you're saying that you'll go back to England and forget all you've done, all you've spent?'

'Isn't that what you want?' he asked coolly.

'No, it's not,' she riposted, frowning at him, wondering whether he'd gone out of his mind. 'Can you afford to throw money away like that?'

'It wouldn't be wasted. MM Charters would remain in good hands—unless, of course, you let your father anywhere near it.'

'I wouldn't allow that to happen, you know that, but neither can I accept the business as a gift.'

'So we're back to square one?' he said several long seconds later, when they had both stood in awkward silence.

At least, it was awkward on Simone's part; she wasn't sure what Cade was thinking or feeling. She lifted her brows and waited, unaware that her wide violet eyes were having a disturbing effect on Cade.

He shook his head, as if trying to rid it of unwelcome thoughts. 'You stay with me until your business is back on its feet, and then I'll return to England and let you lead your life the way you want. But we share the profits. And if you ever need me—for whatever reason, business or personal—all you'll have to do is pick up the phone.'

Simone stood in silence. This was more than she had envisaged. He was being far too generous. Nevertheless, he'd paid a high price for her body. She couldn't imagine any other man making the same kind of deal.

And she was thanking him by keeping their baby a secret!

'I'll leave you to think about it,' said Cade, and even though it killed him to walk away and not take her into his arms, persuade her that all he had at heart was her interests, he knew that he had to do it. Simone had to make the final decision herself. It wouldn't be fair of him to use hot sizzling sex to settle the argument. Which was what he wanted to do.

A few minutes later Simone heard Cade drive away, and only then did she breathe a sigh of relief. She was in an impossible situation. Maybe she should have snapped Cade's hand off and accepted his more-than-charitable offer. At least then he would have been out of her life. He would never know about their child.

Simone halted her thoughts. How cruel would that be? What was she thinking? Of course Cade must know. There was no doubt about it. Nevertheless there had to be a right time to tell him.

On the other hand, warned an inner voice, *you wouldn't want him to commit to you if he doesn't love you.*

No, I wouldn't, she agreed.

She spent a troubled few hours contemplating her dilemma, and then a phone call from her mother pushed all thoughts of it out of her head.

'Simone, your father's in hospital. He's critically ill. You'd best come.'

'Where are you?' asked Simone, shocked when she discovered that her mother was already at the hospital.

'Why didn't you phone me sooner? I would have come for you,' she said disapprovingly.

'It all happened so quickly,' answered Pamela.

Simone assured her that she'd be there as soon as possible, and when she arrived she was stunned to see her father lying pale and still, his eyes closed, his breathing shallow. In contrast her mother looked remarkably healthy, having got over the bug that had laid her low.

'What happened?' she asked quietly as they both sat beside his bed.

'Lily next door phoned to say he'd collapsed and was being taken away in an ambulance. It's drink-related, obviously, his organs have been declining for ages. It was only a matter of time.' Even though Pamela had been forced into a nursing home because of the strain of living with Matthew, her love was still there, and she felt enormously sorry for him.

Simone took her father's hand. It was cold and lifeless, and he had no idea that she was there. How long she and her mother sat with him she didn't know, but she suddenly realised that it was dark, and if Cade was back he would be wondering where she was.

She rang the beach house, but there was no answer, so she tried his mobile phone.

He answered instantly. 'Simone, where the hell are you? I thought you'd changed your mind and gone back to your father's house, but I'm there, and there's no one at home. Your mobile phone's switched off. What the devil's going on?'

'I'm at the hospital,' she explained. 'My—'

'The hospital?' he cut in. 'Why? What's wrong? Have you hurt yourself again?'

'No,' she answered fiercely and instantly. 'It's my father. He's very ill.'

'I'll be there,' he said, and before she could tell him not to bother he ended the call.

Within fifteen minutes he was at the hospital, and her mother insisted that she go outside and talk to him.

'How serious is it?' asked Cade, taking her gently by the shoulders and looking down into her troubled face.

'It doesn't look good,' she answered, and, unable to help herself, she buried her head into his chest. She had never thought that she would cry over her father, but she felt tears trickling down her cheeks, and when Cade offered her his handkerchief she took it gratefully.

His strong arms held her, his voice comforted her, and Simone wondered whether she'd ever be able to cope with life without him. He had filled her every waking moment these last weeks, and she'd realised that the love she'd once felt for him had never gone away. She'd been angry with him, yes, she'd told herself she hated him—but the reality was that he was her one true love.

'He's in the best place,' Cade assured her quietly.

Simone nodded, and after a few minutes they returned to the ward.

Her mother was crying. 'He's gone,' she said. 'He just slipped away.'

It was Simone's turn this time to comfort her mother, and when they finally left the hospital Cade suggested to Pamela that she come and stay with them at the beach house.

But she shook her head. 'I'll be better off in a place I'm familiar with. I have friends at the home. I'm comfortable there. But thank you for asking. And please look after my daughter.'

'You can rest assured on that point, Mrs Maxwell,' he answered. 'And if there's anything at all I can do for you…'

'I know I can call on you,' she said softly. 'You're a good man, Cade.'

Simone knew exactly why her mother had asked him to look after her. In fact, she'd been on tenterhooks in case her parent had let slip her condition.

When they got home, Cade sat Simone down and poured her a small brandy.

'I don't like the stuff,' she protested, but he wouldn't listen.

'It will do you good,' he insisted. 'You're in shock, you have no colour.'

Simone knew that she oughtn't to be drinking in her condition, but he stood over her, so she took a tiny sip to satisfy him. 'I can't believe he's gone,' she said. 'I hated him so much at times, but I'll miss him nevertheless.'

'Of course you will,' reassured Cade. 'It's only natural.'

She wanted to throw herself into his arms again, seek the comfort she needed, but she knew that if she did so she would break down and tell him about the baby, and now wasn't the time. Would there ever be a right time? she wondered.

In the days that followed Cade took over. He organised the funeral. He had cleaners sent into her father's house so that everyone could go back there afterwards. Her mother didn't want any fuss, just something simple at home. So he ordered the food and the drink, despite Simone's protest that she was quite capable of doing it herself.

'You're looking very washed out these days,' he said. 'Your father's death's hit you hard, hasn't it?'

Simone nodded; best to let him think that was the reason for her pale face.

Pamela thought he was marvelous, and Simone couldn't help wondering whether he had an ulterior motive. There had to be something going on in that dark mind of his.

On the day of the funeral Cade never left her side, very much giving the impression to members of her family that they were an item. They all remembered him from years ago, and indeed her Uncle John, her father's brother, asked when they were getting married.

'We're not,' she declared, glancing at Cade. Nevertheless she felt sinful that she was still keeping him in ignorance of her condition.

Later that day, when they'd returned to the beach house and were sitting outside enjoying the cooler evening air, Cade said, 'Does your father's death alter anything?'

Simone frowned. 'I don't know what you mean.'

'You might be thinking of returning to the house.'

'I'll have no choice once—' She stopped abruptly.

'Once what?' he questioned, a deep frown gouging his forehead.

Once you have no further use for me, were the words that crept into her head. But what she said was, 'Once you've gone back to England.'

Cade's lips thinned. 'Is that what you truly want?' And his eyes were frighteningly cold on hers, no longer beautiful, but like two hard, featureless stones.

Simone wished she could see inside his head, find out what he really expected from her. 'Of course it is. Our contract's almost over. There'll be no reason for you to stay here—unless you're going back on your word?'

'And why would I do that?' There was an icy stillness about him now.

'I don't know,' she answered with a shrug. 'Stranger things have happened.'

'I can assure you, Simone, that my word is my bond.'

Simone wasn't sure whether she could believe him. And in actual fact she'd had enough of him today, she needed space. He'd been at her side right from when she'd got up this morning. She was grateful for all he'd done, for the support he'd given her, but enough was enough.

'It's been a long day,' she said. 'I'm going to lie down for a while.'

She felt sure he would insist that she stay and keep him company—either that or he would want to join her—and she was surprised when he did nothing except lift his well-marked brows. It was so unlike the Cade she knew, not to want to share her bed, even if it was only to hold and comfort her. It was almost as though he'd taken her at her word and decided that he'd punished her enough.

Contrarily, she felt disappointed, but she was tired—in fact, she didn't feel at all well—and as she walked back into the house her head began to spin.

'Simone!' Cade jumped to his feet. He saw her falter, saw her slow down and hesitate, saw the hand she clapped to her brow, then he saw her sink slowly to the floor as though her bones had melted and she could no longer stand. All hell broke loose inside him. *'Simone!'* he exclaimed again, but more loudly this time.

By now he had reached her. It was the upset of her father's death and then the funeral that had made her faint, he thought. She'd hardly eaten a thing today; he'd seen her picking at her food.

He carried her indoors and laid her down on his bed. She looked small and defenceless, every vestige of colour drained from her face.

When she opened her eyes, Simone looked around her in a dazed fashion for a few seconds before recovering and shooting up.

'Simone, be careful,' he warned gently. 'You fainted. Let me get you a glass of water.'

By the time he returned, she was sitting on the edge of the bed. 'Did you hurt yourself?' he asked, his brow creased in concern. She looked so pale he was worried.

'I don't think so,' she said quietly.

'You should see a doctor, though,' he asserted, more concerned than he was admitting. 'It's not normal to faint like that.'

'Maybe it is,' she said quietly.

Cade frowned.

Simone dropped her head in her hands. This was make-or-break time. She couldn't keep the news from him any longer, it wouldn't be fair. She'd struggled with her conscience and finally it had won. 'I'm pregnant, Cade,' she said in a voice choked with emotion. Then she waited.

And waited.

Cade's silence was more fearful than if he had raged at her. 'You can't be,' he said at length. 'There's no way.'

'It's true,' she whispered, anguish tying her up in knots.

'How? When? I was always careful.'

'That very first time.'

Cade was silent a moment longer.

'I'm not going to make any claims on you,' said Simone quickly. 'You can go back to England just as you planned. I shall return to my family home. My mother will live with me, and I'll bring the baby up alone.'

'And run the business at the same time?' he snorted. 'You're insane! And I'd be insane to let you. I can't believe this!' And with that he walked out of the house.

Simone let him go. She knew it was a lot for him to take in. It had been a shock for her too. She'd been in denial, just as Cade was now. He needed time to get used to the idea, and she needed space too to decide where her future lay. It was no good staying here; she couldn't possibly sort her mind out while she was living with Cade.

Her mind made up, she quickly packed a bag and drove home. She locked the door behind her and collapsed on to the nearest chair. It was strange here without her father, knowing that he'd never be in this house again, but her life had changed in other ways too. Whether Cade ever became a part of it made no difference. She loved this little person growing inside her more than anything. She constantly wondered whether it was a boy or girl. Not that it mattered—it would be loved just as much either way.

She almost regretted telling Cade now, because she felt sure that he would insist on them marrying—and she didn't want that. She wanted his love first, unconditionally. Maybe she ought to disappear altogether, go somewhere where he would never find her, bring the child up on her own.

Except that she couldn't leave her mother.

Tired as she was, sleep evaded her, and just as she finally managed to drop off someone banged on her door. 'Simone! Open the door! Simone!'

With a groan Simone rolled out of bed and leaned her head out of the window. Cade stood below her on the veranda, looking like a big, angry bear. 'Keep your voice down,' she said. 'You'll wake the neighbours.'

'Then open the door,' he yelled, with little disregard for what she'd said. 'If you don't, I'll break it down.'

Simone pulled on a cotton dressing-gown over her skimpy nightie and reluctantly made her way downstairs. Immediately she turned the key, Cade pushed the door open and stepped inside. He looked as though he'd had as much of a sleepless night as she'd had. 'What do you want?' she asked stonily.

'What do I want?' he echoed, his golden eyes hard on hers.

'Isn't it obvious? I want to know why you haven't told me before about *my* child.'

'Why do you think?' she riposted. 'I knew how you'd react. Fathering a baby was the last thing on your agenda. You probably think I did it deliberately. Well, let me tell, you I didn't. I didn't want anything that would tie me to you for the rest of my life. I'm as sick about it as you are.'

Cade's eyes widened disbelievingly. 'You're telling me you don't want this child? I hope to goodness you're not thinking of—'

'Of course I'm not,' slammed Simone. 'What do you take me for?'

Cade didn't know what to think. He'd just spent the blackest night of his life. A baby! *His* baby! He couldn't believe he'd been so careless. He'd had no plans to become a father, not yet, not for a long time.

But in those dark hours he'd made a startling discovery. One that he had to share with Simone. He wasn't sure, though, whether she'd believe him. She might think he was doing it for the sake of their unborn child. And, even if she didn't love him in return, he felt certain that she would one day. She surely couldn't have given so much of herself to him if there wasn't some feeling there.

Maybe she'd been repressing it, maybe she did love him. She'd have been afraid to tell him, that was for sure, when he'd made no bones about the fact that their relationship was purely a business deal.

He was being a fool. All she'd been doing was making the best of a bad situation. A situation he had created. And he'd let her down. Would she ever forgive him? he wondered. And dared he tell that he loved her?

'We need to talk,' he said.

Simone nodded and led the way through to the family room, where they sat facing the window, looking out at the waterfall cascading down from the pool on the level above.

He knew water always soothed Simone, and he was pleased that she'd chosen to sit here. There was something about water; it was why he loved working with boats, why he loved the beach house so much.

'How long have you known?' he asked, half-turning in his seat so that he could see her face.

Simone closed her eyes. 'A week or so, perhaps. I don't know, I can't remember.'

'And were you ever going to tell me? Or would you have let me return to England never knowing that I was about to become a father?' He tried hard not to allow censure to creep into his voice, but he could hear himself challenging her. And why not? This was an issue far too serious to be nice about. Damn her! She'd had no right keeping this from him.

'I don't know,' answered Simone quietly.

'You don't think that I had as much right to know as you?' he asked harshly. 'Damn it, Simone, what were you thinking? That I'd turn my back on you? I couldn't do that. I'm as much at fault as you. We're in this together, Simone, like it or not.'

When she remained silent, when she looked steadfastly out of the window, he put two fingers beneath her chin and turned her face towards him. He saw fear in her eyes, he saw unhappiness, but he also thought he saw the bloom of motherhood. Or was it his imagination?

Whatever, it reached out to him, it crept into his heart, it filled his whole body with music. He had never in his life felt like this before. Gone was the sharp business mind; in its place was a prospective father, full of love and warmth and optimism.

'Simone,' he said quietly, humbly, even, 'I love you.' The

words slipped out far more easily than he had imagined. Because it was true. He did love her, he always had, though he'd been too foolish and too stubborn to realise it.

Simone's eyes widened in an amazing blaze of violet, her long, thick lashes surrounding them like a beautiful picture-frame. The colour in her cheeks heightened too, and her infinitely soft, kissable lips hung open.

God, he wanted to take them right now, this very second. He could feel his hormone levels rising, his heartrate building, his skin burning. How he stopped himself from kissing her, he didn't know. But from somewhere came the strength to resist.

Simone knew why Cade was saying that he loved her. And it wasn't what she wanted. She wanted him to love her for all the right reasons. 'No, you don't,' she said firmly. 'I don't want you doing the honourable thing. I'll not feel aggrieved if you walk. I wouldn't blame you.'

'You think I'd leave you to go through this alone?'

'I wouldn't be alone, I'd have my mother,' she retorted.

How he loved the fire in her eyes. They were magnificent. Lord, it was hard keeping his hands off her. 'It's not the same thing. I do love you, Simone, I've simply been too blind to see it. How could I take you like I did and not love you? It's not my style, even though I set out to punish you in the beginning. Not in this way, though. Never!'

His beautiful eyes implored her to believe him, his deep voice was gruff with emotion, and Simone could feel herself melting. But she had to be sure. 'If you love me, why have you never told me? Why wait until now?'

'Because I didn't know myself,' he admitted on a sigh. 'It's taken this to bring me to my senses. You're an incredible woman, Simone. I admire your strength. You gave yourself to me to save your business—that must have taken some doing. And you planned to bring up this child without telling me, simply because you didn't want him—or her—to have a father who didn't love their mother. You're very special. Do you think you could ever find it in your heart to love me again? Or have I done irreparable damage?'

It was a long speech for Cade to make, and Simone's heart melted. 'I don't have to look deep into my heart, Cade. I love you. I always have. I'd never have agreed to become your mistress otherwise, no matter how much I wanted to save the family business.'

She watched the emotions crossing Cade's face, incomprehension turning into acceptance, slowly, beautifully. And then they were in each other's arms, kissing, touching, feeling, aware that they had a whole new future ahead of them.

There was much to sort out. Cade's home was in England, hers was here. That could pose a problem. But for the moment Simone didn't care. Cade loved her, she loved him. What else mattered?

'Then, my darling Simone…' Cade was down on one knee. 'Will you do me the honour of becoming my wife?'

'Yes! A thousand times yes.' She launched herself into his arms and, amidst tears and laughter, he kissed her. And it was such a different kiss. This one held promise of a lifetime's happiness, of fun and of laughter, of rearing children, of still being deeply in love into their old age.

They each had so much to offer. How could she have ever let him go, knowing how much she loved him? This child, this baby growing inside her, had formed an indestructible bond between them. It had opened their eyes, made them see what they would be missing.

Now they were one. For ever.

She was the luckiest woman in the world.

'Simone,' said Cade softly and urgently, 'I am the luckiest man alive.'

She smiled. How coincidental was it that he had reiterated her thoughts? Yes, they were both lucky that they'd met again, fallen back in love, and were now being blessed by the tiny life growing inside her. She took Cade's hand and placed it on her stomach. 'This little guy in here is the lucky one. He'll have such a wonderful father.'

'And mother, my sweet. You're sensational. Have I ever told you that? Come—' he stood up and held out his hand '—let us celebrate.'

'I can't drink, Cade, it wouldn't be wise,' she said softly.

'Whose talking about drink? There are more pleasurable ways, my darling, of celebrating. You above all people should know that.' And he led her towards the stairs.

0608 Gen Std HB

JULY 2008 HARDBACK TITLES

ROMANCE

The De Santis Marriage *Michelle Reid*	978 0 263 20318 9
Greek Tycoon, Waitress Wife *Julia James*	978 0 263 20319 6
The Italian Boss's Mistress of Revenge *Trish Morey*	978 0 263 20320 2
One Night with His Virgin Mistress *Sara Craven*	978 0 263 20321 9
Bedded by the Greek Billionaire *Kate Walker*	978 0 263 20322 6
Secretary Mistress, Convenient Wife *Maggie Cox*	978 0 263 20323 3
The Billionaire's Blackmail Bargain *Margaret Mayo*	978 0 263 20324 0
The Italian's Bought Bride *Kate Hewitt*	978 0 263 20325 7
Wedding at Wangaree Valley *Margaret Way*	978 0 263 20326 4
Crazy about her Spanish Boss *Rebecca Winters*	978 0 263 20327 1
The Millionaire's Proposal *Trish Wylie*	978 0 263 20328 8
Abby and the Playboy Prince *Raye Morgan*	978 0 263 20329 5
The Bridegroom's Secret *Melissa James*	978 0 263 20330 1
Texas Ranger Takes a Bride *Patricia Thayer*	978 0 263 20331 8
A Doctor, A Nurse: A Little Miracle *Carol Marinelli*	978 0 263 20332 5
The Playboy Doctor's Marriage Proposal *Fiona Lowe*	978 0 263 20333 2

HISTORICAL

The Shocking Lord Standon *Louise Allen*	978 0 263 20204 5
His Cavalry Lady *Joanna Maitland*	978 0 263 20205 2
An Honourable Rogue *Carol Townend*	978 0 263 20206 9

MEDICAL™

Sheikh Surgeon Claims His Bride *Josie Metcalfe*	978 0 263 19902 4
A Proposal Worth Waiting For *Lilian Darcy*	978 0 263 19903 1
Top-Notch Surgeon, Pregnant Nurse *Amy Andrews*	978 0 263 19904 8
A Mother for His Son *Gill Sanderson*	978 0 263 19905 5

Pure reading pleasure

JULY 2008 LARGE PRINT TITLES

ROMANCE

The Martinez Marriage Revenge *Helen Bianchin*	978 0 263 20058 4
The Sheikh's Convenient Virgin *Trish Morey*	978 0 263 20059 1
King of the Desert, Captive Bride *Jane Porter*	978 0 263 20060 7
Spanish Billionaire, Innocent Wife *Kate Walker*	978 0 263 20061 4
A Royal Marriage of Convenience *Marion Lennox*	978 0 263 20062 1
The Italian Tycoon and the Nanny *Rebecca Winters*	978 0 263 20063 8
Promoted: to Wife and Mother *Jessica Hart*	978 0 263 20064 5
Falling for the Rebel Heir *Ally Blake*	978 0 263 20065 2

HISTORICAL

The Dangerous Mr Ryder *Louise Allen*	978 0 263 20160 4
An Improper Aristocrat *Deb Marlowe*	978 0 263 20161 1
The Novice Bride *Carol Townend*	978 0 263 20162 8

MEDICAL™

The Italian's New-Year Marriage Wish *Sarah Morgan*	978 0 263 19962 8
The Doctor's Longed-For Family *Joanna Neil*	978 0 263 19963 5
Their Special-Care Baby *Fiona McArthur*	978 0 263 19964 2
Their Miracle Child *Gill Sanderson*	978 0 263 19965 9
Single Dad, Nurse Bride *Lynne Marshall*	978 0 263 19966 6
A Family for the Children's Doctor *Dianne Drake*	978 0 263 19967 3

0608 Gen Std LP

MILLS & BOON

Pure reading pleasure™

AUGUST 2008 HARDBACK TITLES

ROMANCE

Virgin for the Billionaire's Taking *Penny Jordan*	978 0 263 20334 9
Purchased: His Perfect Wife *Helen Bianchin*	978 0 263 20335 6
The Vasquez Mistress *Sarah Morgan*	978 0 263 20336 3
At the Sheikh's Bidding *Chantelle Shaw*	978 0 263 20337 0
The Spaniard's Marriage Bargain *Abby Green*	978 0 263 20338 7
Sicilian Millionaire, Bought Bride *Catherine Spencer*	978 0 263 20339 4
Italian Prince, Wedlocked Wife *Jennie Lucas*	978 0 263 20340 0
The Desert King's Pregnant Bride *Annie West*	978 0 263 20341 7
Bride at Briar's Ridge *Margaret Way*	978 0 263 20342 4
Last-Minute Proposal *Jessica Hart*	978 0 263 20343 1
The Single Mum and the Tycoon *Caroline Anderson*	978 0 263 20344 8
Found: His Royal Baby *Raye Morgan*	978 0 263 20345 5
The Millionaire's Nanny Arrangement *Linda Goodnight*	978 0 263 20346 2
Hired: The Boss's Bride *Ally Blake*	978 0 263 20347 9
A Boss Beyond Compare *Dianne Drake*	978 0 263 20348 6
The Emergency Doctor's Chosen Wife *Molly Evans*	978 0 263 20349 3

HISTORICAL

Scandalising the Ton *Diane Gaston*	978 0 263 20207 6
Her Cinderella Season *Deb Marlowe*	978 0 263 20208 3
The Warrior's Princess Bride *Meriel Fuller*	978 0 263 20209 0

MEDICAL™

A Baby for Eve *Maggie Kingsley*	978 0 263 19906 2
Marrying the Millionaire Doctor *Alison Roberts*	978 0 263 19907 9
His Very Special Bride *Joanna Neil*	978 0 263 19908 6
City Surgeon, Outback Bride *Lucy Clark*	978 0 263 19909 3

MILLS & BOON®
Pure reading pleasure™

AUGUST 2008 LARGE PRINT TITLES

ROMANCE

The Italian Billionaire's Pregnant Bride   978 0 263 20066 9
Lynne Graham

The Guardian's Forbidden Mistress   978 0 263 20067 6
Miranda Lee

Secret Baby, Convenient Wife *Kim Lawrence*   978 0 263 20068 3

Caretti's Forced Bride *Jennie Lucas*   978 0 263 20069 0

The Bride's Baby *Liz Fielding*   978 0 263 20070 6

Expecting a Miracle *Jackie Braun*   978 0 263 20071 3

Wedding Bells at Wandering Creek   978 0 263 20072 0
Patricia Thayer

The Loner's Guarded Heart *Michelle Douglas*   978 0 263 20073 7

HISTORICAL

Lady Gwendolen Investigates *Anne Ashley*   978 0 263 20163 5

The Unknown Heir *Anne Herries*   978 0 263 20164 2

Forbidden Lord *Helen Dickson*   978 0 263 20165 9

MEDICAL™

The Doctor's Bride By Sunrise *Josie Metcalfe*   978 0 263 19968 0

Found: A Father For Her Child *Amy Andrews*   978 0 263 19969 7

A Single Dad at Heathermere *Abigail Gordon*   978 0 263 19970 3

Her Very Special Baby *Lucy Clark*   978 0 263 19971 0

The Heart Surgeon's Secret Son *Janice Lynn*   978 0 263 19972 7

The Sheikh Surgeon's Proposal *Olivia Gates*   978 0 263 19973 4